Lizzi
"So how would the news..."

"My family including my grandfather are at present at the island. It belongs to our family, totally private. There would be no press intrusion for you to deal with for the weeks...months."

"So the plan would be?"

"We marry, go there and play the newlyweds until the charade is no longer necessary."

"You're relentless, aren't you?"

"I prefer focused."

"I don't like being organized."

Adonis's lips quirked. "Yes, I am getting that."

"So if I agree, in three months' time I'll be married and separated."

"I thought you already had agreed."

"That's because you only hear what you want to."

He laughed, then adopting a more serious note, added, "Divorce is not a stigma any longer."

"It's not divorce. It's marriage. It's something I always vowed... I never intended to get married, ever."

His brows lifted at her vehemence, then he watched as the frown lines in her forehead smoothed.

"But this wouldn't count, would it?"

Kim Lawrence lives on a farm in Anglesey with her university-lecturer husband, assorted pets who arrived as strays and never left, and sometimes one or both of her boomerang sons. When she's not writing, she loves to be outdoors gardening or walking on one of the beaches for which the island is famous—along with being the place where Prince William and Catherine made their first home!

Books by Kim Lawrence

Harlequin Presents

Claimed by Her Greek Boss
Awakened in Her Enemy's Palazzo
His Wedding Day Revenge
Engaged in Deception

Jet-Set Billionaires

Innocent in the Sicilian's Palazzo

The Secret Twin Sisters

The Prince's Forbidden Cinderella
Her Forbidden Awakening in Greece

Visit the Author Profile page
at Harlequin.com for more titles.

LAST-MINUTE VOWS

KIM LAWRENCE

PRESENTS

Harlequin® PRESENTS™

ISBN-13: 978-1-335-21907-7

Last-Minute Vows

Recycling programs for this product may not exist in your area.

Harlequin Enterprises ULC
22 Adelaide St. West, 41st Floor
Toronto, Ontario M5H 4E3, Canada
www.Harlequin.com

Printed in U.S.A.

LAST-MINUTE VOWS

For people who welcome rescue animals into their homes and hearts, and the real Mouse Cat, and his furry friend Arthur, the very sweetest dog. Sadly, both were no longer with me by the time I finished this book, but they were an inspiration.

PROLOGUE

Two years ago

HEAD DOWN, thinking wistfully of the jacket that in her haste she had left slung over a chair, Lizzie walked straight into a puddle. She was approaching the flight of shallow stone steps that led to the impressive porticoed entrance of the exclusive hotel hosting the meet-and-greet dinner for the two families about to be joined by matrimony. Hosted and paid for by Lizzie's own father.

It was a generous gesture considering the bride was not his daughter but his niece. Although her dad, the head of a successful firm specialising in maritime law, could afford the gesture, and, as he often said, he couldn't have been any more proud of Deb if she had been his own daughter.

Lizzie, who was his own daughter, rarely— actually, never—elicited the same sort of rave reviews from her parent. This had been the case even before her cousin had burnished her already glowing golden child crown by marrying into the Aetos shipping family, who happened to be her dad's most important client.

While her dad had never come right out and said so—he was not an unkind man—Lizzie knew she was a bit of a disappointment. Their relationship had actually improved since she'd stopped trying to win his approval, and she could see his point of view. Unlike her cousin, she was not a professional asset and no one had ever called her dynamic.

As for working the room, her dad frequently forgot she was in the room, a situation that suited Lizzie fine—she didn't like to be the centre of attention.

Swearing softly under her breath, she decided not to look at the puddle damage to her pale-coloured suede heels—the only bit of her outfit that worked—and her spirits lifted a little as she saw a uniformed doorman holding an umbrella rushing forward. Her half-smile withered as he hurried past her to someone he presumably considered more deserving.

Someone who wasn't going to arrive looking like a drowned rat, she thought, adopting a tight-lipped stoic stance as she sidestepped to avoid a couple running down the steps wielding a large brolly like a battering ram.

A snatch of their conversation reached her as they passed by. 'I don't know what you're worrying about…'

The words, though not the supportive intonation, threw her mind back to her last conversation with the bride-to-be. There had been nothing that could be construed as supportive in Deb's voice, just bored irritation as Lizzie had admitted she was really nervous about being her cousin's bridesmaid.

'I don't know what you're worried about. Nobody will be looking at you.' Deb had dismissed Lizzie's comment as she'd tossed her river-sleek silver-blonde hair in a practised flicking action, a complacent smile curving her lips as she'd caught the rippling effect in the wall of mirrors. They had also revealed Lizzie in her mushroom-coloured gown with puff sleeves—she'd looked awful but then she defied anyone to look good in that shade.

'They will if I fall over this walking down the aisle,' Lizzie had pointed out, holding up the acres of drab fabric that had pooled on the carpet.

'Don't be ridiculous. There will be a hem and you won't be wearing heels.'

'I won't?' Lizzie, who stood five two in her bare feet, had responded to this information with a depressed grimace before reminding herself that in this dress no one would see her legs, which, while not supermodel length like her cousin's, were pretty good.

'And I want you as my bridesmaid. You're like my sister.' Deb had pouted, air-kissing either side of Lizzie's face. 'Everyone knows that.'

Actually, not everyone. Just Lizzie's dad.

Lizzie sometimes wondered if her dad really believed they were like sisters or if it was wishful thinking because Deb was the sort of daughter he not so secretly longed for.

It had been her dad who had offered a perfect solution to a single parent's dilemma, when, soon after Lizzie's own mum's premature death, Deb's mum's modelling career had experienced a revival. She had become the face of a global cosmetics brand, upping her profile and offering opportunities that entailed whisking her off to exotic locations around the world.

'Deb can stay with us…she'll be company for Lizzie.'

This arrangement had resulted in the two girls, who were of similar age, being virtually brought up together, and when Deb's glamorous mother had been home Lizzie had often been shunted to their apartment.

They said that opposites attracted but, in the case of Lizzie and her cousin, they really didn't, which was partly why Lizzie had been surprised to be asked to be bridesmaid, but not flattered, after her cousin had explained she didn't want a gaggle of attention-seeking bridesmaids all trying to upstage her.

Lizzie had responded with a thanks, but no, thanks and explained that she didn't feel she was the right fit for the role.

Deb had gone straight to her uncle in tears, heartbroken that Lizzie wouldn't be her bridesmaid.

Her dad had been disappointed.

Deb had continued to be dramatically heartbroken, weeping without ruining her make-up.

What chance did Lizzie have? She could have held out against the pressure but what would have been the point? Better to gracefully concede defeat because she knew that what Deb wanted, she got, especially, historically, if it was something that Lizzie wanted.

Her cousin was very competitive.

The things that Deb had wanted down the years had included the special boyfriend that Lizzie had imagined herself in love with—so much in love and convinced that he was the one, she had brought him home to meet her dad.

Big mistake.

It had taken Deb just a few pouts and head tosses to make him forget that Lizzie existed. Lizzie had pretended that the flirting over dinner between her cousin and boyfriend was just light-hearted. But when she'd set out to see if he had got lost finding his way back from the bathroom, it had been impossible to put a positive spin on discovering her boyfriend enjoying a very close encounter with her cousin on the bathroom floor.

She could nearly laugh about it now.

Well, at least the early and very important lesson had taught her that loving someone gave them the power to hurt you. Lizzie was not keen on being hurt, so during the head-on collision with something that resembled a stone wall she definitely did not enjoy the sensation of having the breath knocked out of her lungs in a soft, shocked whoosh.

The impact caused her to step backwards, and she tensed in anticipation of the inevitable jolting impact of hitting the step below, her arms windmilling wildly cartoon-character style as she sought to regain her balance. But a large hand clamped itself around her forearm, attempting to drag her back onto the step while simultaneously Lizzie reached out, her hand closing around fabric that slipped through her fingers.

A split second later her centre of balance was restored and her hand was cushioned between a much larger hand and a hard, warm, male chest. She could feel the stranger's heart beat and in that odd moment of intimacy felt her own heart rate react, seeming to slow and quicken at the same time, which was, she knew, an impossibility.

'Watch where you're going!'

The voice, velvet, deep, dark, with a gravelly edge that emphasised the terse impatience, shook her free of the weird light-headed moment.

Lizzie shook her head, the impatience in his voice pressing pause on her instinctive apology. The tendency to apologise for everything from the weather to someone standing on her toes was a habit she was trying hard to break.

She tilted her chin and looked up, a long way, as it turned out.

On one hand she was familiar with this face—you'd have to have spent the last years on a desert island not to be—but not familiar in the 'up close and personal' way she now was, near enough to see the faint darker shadow on his close-shaven jaw delineating where stubble would emerge.

Close enough to be uncomfortably aware of his personal forcefield of raw masculinity and conscious all the way down to her curling toes of the overpoweringly earthy, sensual quality he exuded from every perfect pore.

Everything about him in real life was more, from the dramatic symmetry of his carved features, the square jaw, hawkish nose and sharp sybaritic cheekbones, to the heavy-lidded eyes fringed by preposterously long lashes beneath thick, slightly slanted ebony brows and the chiselled sexuality of his mouth, which it was claimed had fuelled a thousand fantasies.

As she took in the healthy glow of his olive-toned skin Lizzie was no longer sceptical of this extravagant claim.

Adonis didn't pause to analyse the strange reluctance he felt to release the small hand pressed to his chest or the fact it took a conscious effort to uncurl his individual fingers as he studied the face turned up to him.

Not a beautiful face, but heart-shaped, and her skin had a startling clarity, a clarity highlighted by the freckles sprinkled over her rounded, smooth cheeks and the bridge of her small nose.

Her kitten eyes, a startling sky blue, were too big, as was her mouth, which was wide, the cushiony full lips almost indecently sensual.

He felt as if he had walked into a wall of mind-numbing lust, something basic and raw—something about that face shook loose a hunger in him. As his eyes sank lower his glance landed on the billowing fabric across her middle and he experienced a flash of sense-cooling reality—the woman was pregnant.

'Are you all right? You really should be more careful in your condition.'

She discovered that the man who had been called the sexiest male on the planet was not looking at her face.

'In my condition?' she began, her voice vague as she struggled free of the weird inertia that chained her to the spot.

She was silently awarding him a brownie point when she realised that he wasn't staring at her boobs—so many men equated the size of a woman's breasts to their sexuality and availability, and hers were not small—his gaze was riveted lower on her middle, where her dress was ballooning in the wind.

His frowning regard returned to her face as he proceeded to lecture. 'In your condition you should take more care.'

Her confusion gave way to dawning horrified comprehension. Did he...? Was it possible he thought she was pregnant? Humiliation pumped through her in a red-hot stream.

Her colour fluctuation alarmed him. He really didn't fancy the idea of having a pregnant woman faint at his feet. 'Are you all right? Do you need to sit down?'

She made a batting gesture, even though he was not making any attempt to touch her. 'Me take care!' she snapped, nostrils flaring. 'I like that! You barged into me. One thing I really hate is people...men...who act like everyone has to get out of their way and are happy to trample on anyone who doesn't! And don't say, "Don't you know who I am?" Because I do and I don't care.'

Taken by surprise, he didn't immediately react to the attack, coming as it did from a totally unexpected diminutive source. During the short static silence that followed her fiery outburst he read the anger and, yes, contempt blazing in her azure eyes.

'I wasn't going to. But good to know.'

The sarcasm and insincerity of his soft response made her teeth ache.

'But actually you bumped into me.' He had no idea if her outburst was the result of an unhinged personality or pregnancy hormones, but his willingness to cut her some slack was limited. He would never normally tolerate being spoken to that way.

'We could debate this,' she tossed back with a haughty sniff, 'but I have better things to do.'

He watched her stalk off, sections of her rich chestnut-brown hair confined in a knot at her nape coming loose and falling down the back of the nightmare of a dress. The aggressive little vixen clearly did not follow the current trend for showing off a baby bump in clothes that clung and celebrated a burgeoning bump.

Pregnant... I do not believe it, she thought, fuming as she stepped inside the gilded entrance hallway.

'And I actually felt sorry for him. Almost,' she mumbled under her breath.

The conversation that had elicited this sympathy replayed in her head as she took a couple of deep steadying breaths and told herself to calm down.

Deb had been force-feeding her the contents of a glossy magazine, reading out all the captions below the photo spread of her and her future husband, along with a detailed description of what she was wearing, name-dropping designers who were falling over themselves to give her freebies because of the Aetos name.

Lizzie had let the words flow over her.

'I was worried about the new colourist…he came highly recommended though.'

'Oh, your hair looks lovely,' Lizzie had said.

'Adonis thought it was a joke when I asked him if he'd ever thought of going a bit lighter.'

'He is very handsome,' Lizzie had conceded, glancing at the man who had stared out from the pages looking moody and broody and quite impossibly gorgeous.

At the time she had told herself that no one was that good-looking and it was the lighting and a few clever filters. Now she knew it wasn't.

She felt a lot less inclined to feel sorry for him now as Deb's response replayed in her head.

'Handsome? Well, obviously I wouldn't marry an ugly man no matter how rich he was. He's not as gorgeous as Luke or Stephan, beautiful boys for fun, but not really keepers.'

It had taken Lizzie several seconds to realise that it wasn't a joke. Her cousin really had been comparing the man she was to marry unfavourably to the pair of clones with blond-streaked highlights and tans that stayed just the right side of orange that her cousin had dated.

Actually, she might not have been putting the right faces to the names—there had been a few others whose names Lizzie couldn't recall. She just remembered that her dad and aunt had been pleased that Deb was getting out there. Their approval was connected, Lizzie suspected, with the nameless married man that her cousin had got involved with in her early twenties.

'I know he's rich, but you don't need his money. You don't have to marry him if you're not in love.'

'You are such a child sometimes, Lizzie. Of course I want to marry him—he is Adonis Aetos. He thinks I'm perfect, which is what counts. Everyone else wanted him and I got him.'

Which, from her beautiful shallow cousin's point of view, was the main thing, hence the fleeting sympathy Lizzie had felt for the groom-to-be. Now, having met him, she felt that they deserved one another.

As Lizzie stalked past a massive gilded mirror, her heart still thudding after her encounter with the tall, rude Greek, she caught sight of herself.

Her anger melted into horror. She looked, she decided, like an inflated balloon about to take off in the mustard-yellow silk—the colour of the season, she had been reliably informed. The cut fell from an elaborately smocked bodice that flattened her boobs and at the same time made them seem even bigger, if such a thing were possible!

She had only herself to blame. She had chosen to believe the perfectly groomed, stick-thin sales assistant who had spoken about unflattering lighting.

She shrugged, her sense of humour coming to her rescue. It was just a dress. If she avoided every reflective surface she might get through tonight, so long as she wasn't arrested by the fashion police.

When it came to things she cared about, Lizzie could and did fight her corner, but when it came to clothes, she didn't care that much, and by the time she had fought her way into this dress she had been standing waist deep in a pile of rejected but safe black and brown— coincidentally cheaper—dresses.

Actually there had been two, but it had felt like a lot, and though Lizzie could have argued the saleswoman's claim that darker colours were really not slimming to larger ladies, by that point she had lost the will to live. Added to which she had already been late for her meeting with the new illustrator so she had taken the line of least resistance, working on the theory nobody was going to be looking at her. This was Deb's evening.

But of course they would be looking and for all the wrong reasons. She lifted her chin, pasted on a smile and thought, *Man up, tomorrow the full frilly horror of it will be donated to a charity shop.* And it wasn't as if it would be her worst fashion mistake. She had form— that had been falling out of her halter-neck bikini playing volleyball on the beach.

She had spent the rest of her holiday in a kaftan while her 'friends'—she'd discovered on their flight that she had only been invited to make up the villa numbers and cut down the cost—had flaunted their flat abs and perky boobs in nearly there bra tops.

This did rate as her most expensive mistake, but then her exasperated rather than generous father was paying, because, as he had said, he didn't want the Aetos family to think she was the hired help.

Actually, Lizzie could have afforded her own expensive clothes had she wanted them. It had yet to dawn on her dad that her 'little hobby' paid.

When her first self-published book—*The Fe-*

line Feminist, a story about the comic romantic disasters of a twenty-something woman written from the point of view of the heroine's cat—had become an overnight success, Lizzie had been as surprised as anyone.

Now there were four books in the series, she had a publisher, an agent, the whole deal and while her dad had pronounced himself happy she had a suitable hobby he had advised her not to do anything foolish like pack in her day job.

Catching sight of a row of tasteful vanity units and mirrors as a door swung open, she detoured. A few minutes spent repairing the damage from the rain to her face and hair would be well spent. Standing in front of the mirror, she patted the frills that made her square shoulders look enormous and took a deep breath, reminding herself that, to quote Deb, no one would be looking at her.

The reality was she could have been a six-foot supermodel, not five feet two, and they still wouldn't be looking at her, not with Deb in the room. Her cousin had the indefinable something that made every other woman invisible.

Deb sparkled.

She was sparkling when Lizzie slipped as unobtrusively as possible into the room where the two families, champagne in hand, were mingling before the formal get-to-know-one-another meal.

Lizzie stuck to sparkling water and the wall, where she blended in with the flocked wallpaper, and stayed there long enough to assess the level of awfulness to expect from the evening. One or two women had gone for floaty, one was even wearing the same colour as Lizzie, but there the similarity ended.

It was in the red zone of her awful monitor.

Across the room Deb was wearing a necklace, presumably the one she had triumphantly told Lizzie was worth a cool million, that glittered around her swan-like neck and was matched by an equally hefty diamond ring on her finger.

She really was living the dream, or at least her dream. All the diamonds in the world would not make Lizzie embrace a life spent as tabloid fodder dodging paparazzi.

Surely no man alive, certainly not the one striding across the room and carrying all eyes with him, would be worth that? She watched the tall figure weaving his way with sinuous grace towards Deb, making Lizzie think of a very well-groomed and outrageously handsome moth flying towards a flame.

The way he moved was riveting, in a 'jungle

cat stalking its prey way' riveting. You didn't want to watch, but you couldn't not!

The people who weren't staring at Deb were, like Lizzie, watching her future husband, Adonis Aetos, the heir to a Greek shipping fortune, his dark hair with the distinctive widow's peak pushed back from his broad bronzed forehead.

His carved features had been called perfect, the high sharp cheekbones, the planes and hollows so symmetrical they could have made him look effeminate, especially when you considered—as many did—the lush sensuality of his full upper lip, but he wasn't. He was undiluted raw masculinity.

Her stomach flipped as she remembered the charge she had felt when she had been staring into those eyes, before he had assumed she was pregnant.

She watched a possessive arm claim Deb's waist as her cousin tilted her beautiful head to receive the kiss on her cheek. He murmured something that made Deb's silvery laughter ring out.

'Lizzie, I need to go powder my nose.'

Lizzie gave a start and plastered on a smile to greet her godmother, who was examining her dress.

'Your dear mother had such excellent dress sense,' she bemoaned.

Lizzie, who expected nothing less than brutal honesty from her elderly relative, kept smiling.

'I need the ladies' room. Come with me,' her godmother said imperiously. 'You could do with doing…something to your hair.'

It was ten minutes before Lizzie slipped back into the champagne reception through one of the arches that led into the chandelier-lit space, her hair looking pretty much as it had done when she'd left.

She stopped dead. A few feet ahead of her stood her cousin and Adonis Aetos. They remained oblivious to her presence.

An image formed in her head of her stepping forward and revealing herself, cool, composed, hand outstretched.

The image stayed where it was. A better option, she decided, was backing quietly out, less a cowardly retreat and more conserving her energy. Tonight would be an endurance event.

She had not put her slip-away strategy into action before Adonis's deep distinctive voice reached her.

'Your cousin, the one you invited to be your bridesmaid?'

'Poor darling Lizzie. We are more like sisters.'

'She works with you in the family firm?' Lizzie heard him ask in the same casual off-hand voice.

'God, no, darling Uncle tried, bless. He gave her all the opportunities.' She gave a theatrical sigh that made Lizzie's fists clench, her nails digging into her palm. 'But you know how it is with some people—they have no staying power. She only lasted a week.' Another sigh. 'But it's sometimes that way with these little mousey people—they have no drive. Seriously, she is scared of her own shadow. I hate to say it—'

But you're going to say it anyway, Lizzie thought.

'I'm afraid she is just your typical little rich girl. Her daddy pays all her bills, her rent, the lot. I think she does some voluntary sort of stuff. Oh, she's very mousey, and apparently she dreams of being a writer. Don't we all, darling?'

'Mousey?'

From where she stood Lizzie could see his dark brows draw into a straight line above his masterful nose.

'Have I got the right woman, the tiny one in the yellowy tent?'

Deb laughed at the description. 'Oh, God, yes, the dress. Lizzie and fashion are not really friends. She favours the tent. They are usually black though, or, if she is being very frivolous, navy or brown. I've tried to encourage her to make the best of herself.'

'I realise you are fond of her, but, honestly, do you think it's a great idea to have a pregnant woman as your bridesmaid? She might give birth in the church.'

Deb's mirthless cruel cackle made Lizzie wince. Her mustard-encased boobs swelled against the tight fabric as she took a wrathful breath. 'She isn't pregnant, darling. She's just... how can I say it tactfully...?' she purred as she reached up and stroked his lean cheek. 'Stout?'

As Adonis emerged from Deb's long lingering kiss, he looked across her shoulder and found himself staring directly into the bright burning blue gaze of the mousey cousin.

If looks could kill, he'd be lying stone cold and very dead on the floor, a mouse's claws in his vital organs.

If it had been a scene in a drama, she would have undergone a Cinderella transformation, losing twenty pounds and returning midway through the film to have her revenge on the man who had humiliated her by making him fall desperately in love with her. Obviously, she would have rejected him and he would have crawled away a broken man.

The triumph she built in her imagination crumbled as reality kicked in. This wasn't a drama. It was real life and she was not a teenager who believed in fairy tales.

She had believed in fairy tales longer than most—she had still believed in them the day she went to buy her first bra, a long-awaited event as she'd been a late developer.

She remembered the fluttery feeling of excitement when she had spotted the rows of pretty lacy bras that her cousin had headed for. But her aunt had ushered her past the colourful racks to another row without any colour or lace, to what she had explained were minimiser bras, which she had reassured Lizzie would reduce her by a full cup size.

In the real world she wouldn't be losing any weight, partly because according to the charts she inexplicably wasn't overweight, and partly because she enjoyed food. She turned her back on the happy couple and accepted a canapé.

CHAPTER ONE

ADONIS STEPPED OUT of the shower and shook his head, pushing his fingers through the drenched strands of his dripping ebony hair. A quick glance in the steamed-up mirror told him it was time for a trim—the waves were damply curling on his neck in a way he found irritating.

Quickly drying off, he had pulled on a pair of boxers and was reaching for his razor when his phone rang. He saw the caller ID and picked it up, a half-smile curving his mobile, sensually sculpted lips.

'Thought you didn't get up before noon on vacation, Jack.'

'It's hard work to maintain the illusion I'm an entitled hedonist.' His friend's languid response, accompanied by an exaggerated yawn from the workaholic lawyer, drew an ironic grin from Adonis. 'I thought as your best friend, possibly only friend—'

'Thanks for that,' came the dry interruption.

'It takes a very determined person to get past your iron ring of security, and of course your trust issues. Not everyone has an angle, you know.'

Adonis grunted, thinking, No, but most people do.

'But back to the reason I called—it was of course to congratulate you? I'm kind of hurt that I am the last to know.' There was an audible question mark in the light teasing response.

Adonis looped a towel around his neck and walked over to the glass wall of his penthouse apartment, rubbing a hand across the dark stubble on his jaw as he glanced from the numbers on the screen of the laptop set up on his desk to the iconic view of the city far below.

'Last to know what?' His dark brows twitched into a frown. Had someone leaked information on the deal he had spent the last month putting together?

'About your marriage plans. Have you set a date yet?'

Adonis's eyes narrowed. He was not very amused by the joke, particularly given the significance of the date.

Two years ago today he had been meant to be exchanging vows with his beautiful bride.

And Deb had been beautiful, he thought, an

image of her face floating into his head along with a wave of genuine sadness. She'd had her whole life ahead of her. She'd had everything, including him.

An ironic, self-mocking smile tugged at the corners of his mobile lips. Beautiful Deb had taken him for a fool, a fact that he had not discovered until after her death when, along with the helicopter pilot, a third body had been found in the wreckage.

Identified as an older man, neither wealthy nor influential, a married man, and, it turned out, her long-standing lover. This fact was not general knowledge, though how his grandfather had buried that little pearl he didn't know. He must have pulled in one hell of a lot of favours, which meant that the world didn't know that Adonis was a fool. But he did.

His pride had taken a massive hit when he'd discovered he'd been played.

The rumours of his infallibility, he conceded with a cynical grimace, had been grossly exaggerated.

The fact he had been confident that she would have been faithful seemed beyond laughable. It was even more disturbing that in his arrogance he had so readily accepted her word when they had struck their very civilised bargain. Which seemed, in hindsight, irredeemably stupid.

If Deb had actually produced the one child they had agreed on when they had hammered out the details of their practical, mutually beneficial arrangement, which was obviously no means a given, there was a big doubt that any child would have been his.

But that was academic. There was no wife, no child, not even an ignominious divorce. He'd been blinded less by her beauty than by the fact he had been utterly convinced he had found his version of the perfect bride: beautiful, ambitious, driven, and not clingy or, most importantly, in love with him. A fact she had quite happily admitted when he had initially thrown the idea of marriage out there.

He'd been upfront, said he wasn't in love with her, and had had his instincts rewarded when she'd told him that that was not an issue.

She had not recoiled in horror at the possibility of divorce if things were not working, and he'd congratulated himself on finding his perfect bride. For many people, marriage was about staying together and raising kids. For Adonis the staying together aspect was deeply unrealistic, but kids?

He would have happily stayed single but his

grandfather's influence on his younger self meant he was fully aware that it was his duty to provide an heir to continue the Aetos legacy and family name. Of course, it was possible to father a child outside marriage, but it remained a fact of life that legally a marriage contract made a father's rights a lot more secure.

He had never been looking for a woman who thought she was his soul mate—the last thing Adonis wanted in his life was the sort of love that his devoted parents shared.

The sort of romantic love that to his mind had more in common with an obsession than a partnership, mutual obsession that led to emotional stormy fights, and equally emotional making up. As a child he had learnt never to relax. The most peaceful moment could without warning become full-scale no-holds-barred vicious war.

And he had been in the middle. Some of his earliest memories were of being asked to side with one or the other in their current row. He much preferred the times when they had forgotten his existence, sometimes literally.

He had been glad when they'd packed him off to boarding school at seven, arriving with what he'd considered an advantage: he hadn't spent the first weeks crying because he'd missed his parents. There had been weeks before school when Adonis had seen more of hotel staff than his parents, though he had found the food at school not up to the standard of the room service offered by the five-star hotels his parents favoured and he'd spent a great deal of his young life living in.

After he had exchanged hotels for school, he had been offloaded on his grandfather and extended family, spending his holidays on the family's private island, which had suited all involved. While his parents had drifted from one fashionable watering hole to another being beautiful in love people, he'd run wild on the island while being taught the responsibilities that came with being an Aetos, along with privileges that he should never take for granted.

He had nothing against beautiful things or people. He could see the attraction of beautiful... Deb's exquisite face floated into his head. He fully appreciated the irony now that he had been impressed when she'd countered his honesty with some of her own, admitting quite openly that, being married to him, she would enjoy the status and, she was sure, the sex too.

'And on that note... I'm sure the sex will be great, but considering this is a contract situation I'd prefer to wait until the ink is dried?'

He hadn't liked the idea, even for him her attitude was clinical, but he could see the logic. It wasn't as if he'd wanted to stake his claim, own her the way his father wanted to own his mother and vice versa.

At least he hadn't loved her. How could a man who didn't believe in the existence of love find himself a victim of it? He wasn't congratulating himself—being a victim of his own arrogance and lack of judgment was not something to celebrate.

He had messed up big time, but he wouldn't be repeating his error, and he wasn't going to be pressured into marriage, despite his grandfather's growing frustration.

His friend interrupted his chain of thought, pulling him back into the moment. 'So was it a secret? It isn't any more.'

'Enough with the cryptic clues, Jack…get to the punchline. I have a meeting in an hour. I'm not on holiday.' He closed the laptop lid with a decisive click.

'No punchline, no joke. I have the proof in my hand.' The rustle of paper echoed down the line, along with laughter. 'Imagine my surprise when I stumbled across this. And I suspect it won't just be me that stumbled. The notice of the engagement that the families are happy to announce between Mr Adonis Athan—you kept that quiet—Aetos to Miss Elizabeth Rose Sinclair.'

His phone was wedged to his ear as he entered the walk-in wardrobe and selected one of the suits that hung there. 'I don't even know any Elizabeth Rose Sinclair.'

'The daughter of Rafe Sinclair?'

In the act of selecting a tie, he paused. 'Rafe Sinclair? He has a daughter?' Which made her Deb's cousin. A face floated into his head, big kitten eyes, rounded cheeks, a pointy little chin, that mouth… The so-called mouse with a spark of molten anger in her eyes, the die-a-painful-death glare.

Not his idea of a mouse. Was she feeling the pinch now her father's finances were in a death spiral? Was that what this was about? Was she looking for another source of income to replace Daddy? he speculated grimly.

His thoughts continued to fly as he grabbed a fresh shirt and stalked back into his bedroom.

'She is…was Deb's bridesmaid, or she would have been.'

Instead the next time, the last time, he had seen her, had been at the funeral. Wearing a black tent, she had walked right up to him, her eyes huge in her pale face. Like her cousin, she did sincerity very well. Her lips had quivered as she had delivered the formal platitude.

'Sorry for your loss.'

The rest of the time she had been supporting her father. Someone had had to be—Rafe Sinclair had seemed on the point of collapse—and now it seemed the supportive daughter was part of some sort of plot to trap Adonis into marriage. Obviously she hadn't been working alone. He could see his grandfather's fingerprints all over this and, considering his financial woes, her father's also. How complicit was his new bride? he speculated, his lips twisting into a cynical smile.

He was angry.

He was curious.

Had his new bride been aware when they'd met that her cousin had had a married lover tucked away? Was that what had given her the audacity to think he would fall for this sort of obvious trick?

'So I am engaged. Interesting… Thanks for the heads up. Speak later.' He hung up.

His next call went direct to his PA, who was in charge of his carefully choreographed life. She didn't let him get a word in before she launched into a litany of exclamations.

'Engaged! Why didn't you tell me? I've been inundated and I don't even have a quote!'

He cut her off. 'Cancel the meeting.'

'Cancelled.'

'Maybe cancel my day, Jenna.'

'Is it true?'

Adonis, sifting the possibilities in his head, continued to keep his options open. 'That remains to be seen.'

Lizzie was running late. She twisted her thick hair into a loose knot and pinned it on her head, ignoring the thick waving strands that escaped to cluster around her face, without even glancing in the mirror.

She snatched the slice of buttered toast she hadn't got around to eating and glanced automatically at her phone before she slid it into her bag.

The sight of the number of missed calls and messages made her dark feathery brows twitch.

'No time now,' she muttered, narrowly avoiding tripping as her annoyed cat wound herself around Lizzie's legs demanding attention. Not proof against the animal's pathetic miaow and reproachful stare, she paused to pour some dried food into the half-full bowl.

'You're getting fat.'

KIM LAWRENCE   39

The cat gave her an eloquent 'look who's talking' superior feline glare, and walked away from the bowl, tail twitching.

Her phone rang. She saw her dad's number and ignored it. She'd ring back later. Actually she'd been a bit concerned he'd cancelled their last Sunday lunch, which since she'd left home had become an established tradition, and the last time she'd seen him he'd not interrogated her on her love life or lack of it. He'd also told her she looked nice, which was as unusual as it was untrue.

Glancing at the time on her phone before she slid it back into her bag, she debated whether to ring and warn the stables she'd be a few minutes late before deciding it would be quicker just to get a move on.

Her dad approved her work ethic and also approved that she had kept her day job. Approval was relatively rare from her parent so she had not bothered telling him that she now helped at the disabled riding stables where she had worked since leaving school on a voluntary basis. She might not be getting paid but that was no excuse in her mind for bad time-keeping.

Her cottage had an upside-down arrangement, the open-plan living area upstairs and the two bedrooms and bathroom downstairs. She flew down those stairs, hitching her bag over her shoulder as she flung open the front door of her red-brick Victorian terraced cottage.

Normally she would step out onto the path between the tiny square of lawn and the fragrant lavender-lined border, except there was no lawn and her lavender was crushed. There was just a sea of bodies and faces. The sea stretched beyond her garden and onto the street, where more faces were creating a wall of noise.

Disorientated and confused, she stood there blinking as questions came at her from all sides. Like a trapped animal, she half turned and glanced back at her front door, which was now hidden by a jostle of bodies who had moved in all around her, essentially cutting her off from any avenue of escape.

Lizzie hated crowds. Panic flared in her belly as she fought her visceral response, the horrid impression that she was suffocating under the press of bodies, the same way the coats had been pressing in on her when Deb had 'accidentally' locked her in that wardrobe.

'Excuse me, please, I think you've got the wrong person. Excuse me…' Polite having failed, head down, she tried to elbow her way forward taking small shuffling steps. It was like fighting a living tide.

Nothing she said made any impact, nothing paused, nothing stopped—if anything the bodies pressed in closer, not respecting anything resembling personal space. Lizzie, who had massive issues with claustrophobia, focused on her breathing and struggled to slow her hyperventilation as a rash of red dots danced and whirled dizzily in front of her eyes.

She had never fainted in her life... This would be a very bad time to start.

'I'm from the...'

'Exclusive story...'

'Where's the ring, Lizzie Rose?'

Her eyes darted from left to right, stilling as they located a figure who was head and shoulders above the crowd. He moved with a negligent broad ease through the packed bodies, his face hidden by the tinted visor of a helmet.

She had been watching his progress but it was a tummy-flip moment of shock when he appeared at her side. She didn't react when his hand closed around her arm, her eyes just slid from the point of contact upwards. It seemed like a long way upwards. He was very tall, broad-shouldered and athletically lean.

She found herself looking at her own reflection in the visor of the helmet he was wearing. All that was visible of his features was a strong jaw and a sensually sculpted wide mouth.

As she stared up at him for the space of several frantic heartbeats the clamour and the frenzied mob seemed to retreat, unable to compete with the stranger's overwhelming presence.

She had no idea how many seconds ticked by before she shook herself free of the weird thrall.

'I didn't order anything,' she said apologetically as her temporary respite from the babble ended.

Adonis, who had never been mistaken for pizza delivery before, swallowed the unexpected rumble of laughter he felt in his throat.

'If you want to get out of this, come with me.'

Maybe it was his unrealistic confidence that she reacted to, but he was offering her an escape, whereas previously she hadn't been able to move. The crowds seemed to part as, with his hand in the small of her back, they moved through the small garden and onto the street.

They were still surrounded and now she was not the only focus of the stream of questions, though Lizzie didn't take in anything other than the name.

'Adonis... Adonis... Adonis!'

'Did love grow from your mutual grief?'

'When did comfort turn to passion?'

Clamped to his side, not because of any pressure on his part but because of the shelter it offered, Lizzie turned her head. Yes, the jawline was unmistakable and the mouth that had fuelled a million fantasies... Adonis Aetos. Of course it was!

To retain her composure and not be fatally distracted by the hard male muscle or the warm male scent that was making her stomach quiver, she trained her eyes on her toes until they reached the edge of the pavement.

Where now?

Her question was soon answered.

'Oh, God!'

Instinct, not always practical, made her close her eyes as he stepped without hesitation off the pavement, taking her with him. If the lorry didn't get her, the double-decker bus behind it definitely would.

She reached the other side of the road while the bus was just rumbling past.

'Move, woman!' A helmet was shoved unceremoniously in her hand.

She bit back a retort, her eyes narrowing to angry blue slits as she resisted the temptation to tell him where he could shove the damned thing.

People got her wrong sometimes just because she took the road of least resistance when nothing was at stake that she cared about. That did not mean she was in any way pliable. She might look like a brown mouse—no one had called her that since she left school—but she wasn't one.

It could on occasion work to her advantage when people underestimated her. She didn't think this was one of those occasions.

'Get on!'

As the bus trundled along, the mob waiting to cross was revealed. Lizzie decided it was not the moment to argue so she hastily pulled the helmet on and climbed onto the gleaming monster of a motorbike.

'Hold on.'

He didn't even bother with polite pretence. It was an order.

She looked at the leather-clad back of the man in front of her and, holding her breath, she tensed the same way she would have if she was about to duck her head under cold water.

A small yelp was wrenched from her throat as, with a roar, they pulled away from the kerb.

Underneath the leather he was hard and lean.

She was riding pillion with Adonis Aetos.

Could be she was still asleep?

If so, it was a very realistic dream or rather a continuing nightmare.

The cliff-edge emotions she struggled to keep in check surged, sending her thoughts into a flashback moment of childhood terror, when the hide and seek game had left her locked in a wardrobe with no Narnia behind the coats when Deb had forgotten they were playing.

Escape from the memory was not much better. She was bombarded with sensations, her palms damp, her heart pounding, fingers laced tightly into the strap of her bag, digging into her damp palms. She pressed her cheek against his leather-clad back and screamed as he rounded a corner at what felt to her a ridiculous, actually reckless, speed.

She heard, or rather felt, his laugh and bit her lip, determined not to offer him any more opportunities to mock her, when he took a sharp right down a narrow cobbled alley, navigating a number of obstacles at a pace that made her teeth rattle.

It would have been an exaggeration to say that she relaxed as the journey progressed, but she moved beyond the conviction she was going to fall off or die. She refused to acknowledge the zing of exhilaration the combination of speed and hard male body shook loose inside her, and as her thoughts moved beyond survival, other thoughts rushed in to fill the vacuum.

She was clinging not because she was afraid of falling but because she liked the male scent of him, the heat of his lean muscled body filling her senses, blocking out everything else.

Doubtless she was living a lot of women's fantasies. She took a sense-cooling moment to remind herself that this was not her fantasy.

He was rude and arrogant, but annoyingly her dislike was complicated by the fact she felt sorry for him. He had lost the love of his life!

At least he'd had a love.

She didn't envy him. It was an awful thing to lose the person you loved. She'd been twelve when her mum had died, not suddenly but slowly, losing a little part of herself every day.

Early onset Alzheimer's was rare and very cruel. At the time Lizzie hadn't known that. She had just known that her mum, her best friend, the person she loved with a childish ferocity, was dying.

She hadn't known it was her mum who had made her feel safe, secure in the knowledge that she was her Lizzie Rose. The most important person in the world to her. The one person she knew would always be in her corner no matter what.

She hadn't known that until her mum was gone. Not on the day they buried her, that person was gone long before, but Lizzie had still loved her.

She had discovered young that loving came at a price and it was one Lizzie wasn't sure she wanted to pay. The popular theory was you didn't have a choice about falling in love, but Lizzie didn't buy into the what the heart wants mantra.

She had vowed to disprove this theory, and so far she had.

She had never been in love.

Obviously she'd felt sexual attraction, but she'd not allowed it to go farther… Why risk it?

When people said it was 'better to have loved and lost' she thought of her mum, felt everything her twelve-year-old self had felt, and murmured, 'I really don't think so.'

Adonis waited until he was sure he had lost the couple of journalists who had stayed with them following in cars. Even then he did not head directly, instead he took a circuitous route, to the building that housed his penthouse apartment. It was possible there might have been a reception committee and that some enterprising journalist would have beaten him there but this proved not to be the case.

He drove directly into the gated underground parking area, where he pulled his bike into its allocated space between his cars before he dismounted.

With far less elegance, hardly surprising considering the disparity in their leg length, and the fact her knees were shaking, Lizzie followed suit.

She staggered slightly, righted herself and looked around before unfurling her fingers from around the strap of the bag she still clutched in one hand. She flexed her numb white fingers to encourage the blood flow before she dropped the bag and pulled the helmet off. After a tussle she managed it, though the last of the pins her hair had been confined by came with it, leaving her hair to spill untidily down her back.

Adonis's eyes followed the spectacular progress of the rich chestnut-brown waves that bounced softly as they uncoiled, framing the creamy pallor of her pixie-chinned heart-shaped face.

'Where are we?'

Her voice, quiet, soft and surprisingly low, had a breathy catch. At least she wasn't having hysterics, which was a plus, but then her shock horror might have been an act...even though he would have sworn it was real, so real it had kicked him into protective instincts he hadn't known he possessed.

Luckily he no longer went solely on his instincts.

'I live here. Don't worry, there is security, the building is gated, and, besides, I lost them.'

'And I nearly lost my breakfast,' she told him, thinking it would have been almost worth it to see how he coped with that situation.

He winced at the rather literal admission.

'Lost who?'

'The press pack who followed us.'

'Why?'

His shrug, the unconvincing dumb act, fed Lizzie's growing exasperation.

'Why were they there? Why were they following me? Why did they think—?' She couldn't go on. It seemed too crazy a question to voice but there was no escaping the things she had heard.

Below the visor his lips curled. 'You don't know?' he said, loosening the strap on his helmet.

She looked at him, really resenting his tone,

his attitude. Him! 'How would I know? But you appeared. You knew what was happening,' she accused.

He laughed. 'So you don't have a clue… You are just an innocent bystander?' he suggested, not bothering to hide his scepticism.

'Sure, I invited that mob to breakfast. What can I say?' Sarcasm thinly disguised her growing antagonism.

'So you had no idea at all?' he pressed.

'Oh, for God's sake. You can be as sarcastic as you like, you can sneer as much as you like, but it doesn't alter the fact that I don't have the faintest idea what you are talking about,' she finished on a breathless quiver of sheer frustration.

'If there is a conspiracy, no one has filled me in on it!' she yelled, not much caring by this point if her response thickened the tension in the air or his sneery hostility. 'And I am not going anywhere until you tell me what the hell just happened!'

He studied her face for a moment before giving an almost imperceptible nod.

'Not here,' he said tersely. 'Let's carry this discussion upstairs… My apartment,' he added as she looked back at him with eyes that were brilliantly blue and even more unrealistically so than Deb's. Did she wear the same lenses that Deb had and exchange them for green to match her outfits?

'Not possible, just explain what just happened, and why it happened. I need to get to work.'

His dark brows lifted at her peremptory tone. 'You work?' He didn't bother to disguise his scepticism.

'I volunteer at a stables,' she said, explaining the basics.

Pretty much confirmed what Deb had suggested. She lived in a house that Daddy paid for—the property prices in that exclusive little enclave did not come cheap—and she brushed horses. Also, her mouth was not made for pursing.

It was made for kissing. He pushed away the unhelpful observation while noting the fact the lush, pouting curve appeared to be an untouched natural rosy pink.

Did any female not wear any make-up at all? Not any he knew, but he had to admit Elizabeth Rose Sinclair could get away with it and then some. Her skin had a Celtic creamy pallor marked only by a designer sprinkling of freckles across the bridge of her small straight nose and softly rounded cheeks.

Lizzie could feel the prickles of antagonism under her skin as she replayed the disdainful note in his voice, but she could not prioritise her desire to tell him to stuff it because she needed him to unravel the mystery.

What had made the media mob assume that…? God, it was too crazy. She couldn't even think it, let alone say it! She felt as if she had just fallen down the proverbial surreal rabbit hole, and she hadn't reached the bottom.

She really needed some help here. It wasn't just the gaps she needed filling in, it was the entire thing. There were too many hows and whys in her head to count!

'So what's going on?' she asked, telling herself that the answer would make her laugh and not really believing it. 'You didn't roll up in leather like a modern-day knight by accident?'

As she paused for breath she realised that the surreal events were catching up on her in a physical way… Suddenly she could feel the crushing pressure of the baying mob, her dry mouth meant she had to moisten her lips every few seconds and the little internal tremors as she watched Adonis Aetos bend to remove his helmet were a big obstruction to calm, logical reasoning.

This logic bypass was probably the reason

she couldn't stop cataloguing his perfect features. It was an embarrassing compulsion but at least she wasn't being too obvious—he was standing in profile and couldn't see her ogling.

Was it his good side?

She seriously doubted he had a bad side, with the broad forehead, the chiselled cheekbones, strong jaw and the mouth that had launched a million fantasies.

His glossily abundant raven-dark hair was ruffled sexily, standing up in spikes on his perfectly shaped skull. The carved angles and strong planes, the dark stubble on his chin and jaw, added to the air of danger he exuded.

She blinked away the fanciful thought. Danger, she reminded herself—some things couldn't be said too often—could not be attractive. This fact established, she was shaking her head, not ogling like a sad pathetic creature, when he turned his head sharply, possibly sensing her scrutiny.

His night-sky eyes really did have silver flecks... Where had she read that?

One brow lifted. 'After you...' With an elegant flicking motion of his long brown fingers he gestured to the doors of a lift she had previously not noticed.

It was as if he had not heard her at all.

Lizzie could take being tuned out by her family but enough was enough. There had to be a cut-off point. Tension added extra rigidity to her spine as impatience mingled with trepidation and she pulled herself up to her full and deeply unimpressive five two.

'Just tell me,' she said, refusing to be ushered anywhere. His expression suggested that he had never had any woman refuse the invite to his apartment before, though the invitation on those occasions would have been issued in very different circumstances.

His frown reflected his momentary confusion, the confusion of man who was accustomed to people falling in with his wishes.

'You are being—'

In a voice that was deliberately slow and calm she cut across him. 'I have never seen how sitting down and having a cup of tea makes bad news better, and it doesn't take a genius to see nothing you are about to say is going to make me break out into spontaneous joyous song.' By the time she paused to catch her breath, calm and deliberate had become shrill and emotional.

As the breath she tried to catch remained out of reach she pressed a hand to her chest. The tightness felt like an iron fist as she struggled, fighting for oxygen, but not panicking.

She recognised the symptoms, unlike the very first time she had experienced the claustrophobic chest tightness.

Hand shaking, she dipped into her bag and pulled out an inhaler. Fitting it to her lips, she breathed as deep as she could, once, then again, and felt the tightness lessen almost immediately.

Panic over, she waited, arms folded, for him to respond.

'Are you OK?'

'OK?' she echoed, not appreciative of the concern in his voice. 'Who the hell would be OK after this morning? But if you mean…?' She waved her inhaler at him before realising what he was referring to and slipping it back into her bag. 'Oh, I have asthma—mild asthma.'

Adonis didn't buy into the mild, neither did he underestimate how serious asthma could be. He still remembered the kid in his dormitory who had been blue-lighted to intensive care in the middle of the night. He'd never come back and for the rest of the term Adonis had thought he'd died. It wasn't until the next term that he'd discovered the boy's parents had decided to take him home.

'What triggers it?'

Lizzie stared at him, thinking, *Are you serious?* 'Actually a few things, but now I can add a white-knuckle ride on a motorbike driven by a raving lunatic.' She omitted the being pressed up close and personal to a virile male body.

Startled by the less than flattering description, he laughed, his austere expression melting into a grin in the blink of an eye.

He had a sense of humour and an incredibly attractive grin that made him look years younger. Lizzie's own sarcastic smirk faded as she fought the urge to join in his laughter. She was almost relieved when he stopped looking human and frowned accusingly.

'You should have said,' he reproached.

'Oh, yes, I start every conversation with, "And by the way I have asthma." Don't be ridiculous. So, no, I am not OK. I am very not OK.'

'So I take it you did not find the ride exhilarating?'

'Exhilarating?' She snorted, choosing to forget the illicit thrill and instead directing a withering look at him. 'I am not some sort of weird adrenaline junkie. I was terrified!' she retorted. 'You know—in-fear-of-my-life terrified?'

In reality the ride had been nothing compared to the cumulative effect of the media frenzy followed by the close intimate contact with a man who had received a double dose of pheromones.

He looked mildly amused. 'You were never in any danger. Obviously if I had known you had health issues I would have made allowances.'

'I don't have "health issues",' she said, framing the words in angry inverted commas. 'And I don't want or need any allowances from you.'

'Yes, I am getting that.'

It wasn't the only thing he was getting. Adonis was getting the militant sparkle in her narrowed, rather spectacularly blue eyes and the stubborn set of her jaw.

He'd expected her to be either another, slightly more subtle and therefore more dangerous version of her cousin, capable of conniving in this scam. Or innocent, shy, and overwhelmed, perhaps unable to believe her luck to have her name linked with his. Over the years there were enough women who had tried many and varied means of achieving this, some quite inventive.

The pursuit could have left a man believing that he was irresistible had that man believed that his attraction lay in his smile or his charming personality, but Adonis had not fallen into the trap of believing his own PR machine. He was well aware that it was his image, his life-style and his money that made him irresistible. Yet had not fate and a design error that had grounded the entire fleet of helicopters inter-vened, he would have married Deb, who had wanted nothing from him but his money and lifestyle while she carried on an affair with her lover.

'But I would like an explanation and please don't make a big song and dance about that. I simply don't like motorbikes.'

It was impossible to miss the silent addition of 'Or you' that her blue eyes were messaging.

'As modes of transport in the City go, it is a good way—'

'The only place for high-speed chases, in my opinion, is on a cinema screen.'

He laughed and, to her irritation, managed to look even more gorgeous. 'That was not a high-speed chase. I didn't break any speed limits.'

She'd never had much sympathy for women who were attracted to men with a bad-boy per-sona, but for the first time she felt some sympa-thy as she watched, exasperated by her inability not to, as he unzipped his leather jacket to reveal a white tee shirt that was fitted enough to hint at the corrugated flatness of his belly.

She felt the heat curl low in her belly and countered the shame by rushing into accusing speech.

'You were there, you knew this was going to happen...' Her lashes swept downwards before fluttering up again as she fixed him with a suspicious blue accusing stare. 'How could that be, if you didn't plan it?' She shook her head. That sounded even more crazy than it had in her head.

'We should discuss this situation calmly and in private in my apartment.'

Her social mask refused to stay in place. 'Don't patronise me. You know what happened. You knew it was going to happen. You weren't just passing, so tell me.' She stopped short of stamping her foot but only just. It had been a long and very confusing morning.

'Calm down... You'll give yourself another attack,' he said, concealing his genuine concern behind irritation that was genuine too.

'I happen to be perfectly calm.' His laugh made her push the helmet she was still holding towards him hard. 'And this is yours.'

He pulled it into his stomach, his fingers grazing hers. Lizzie froze, her eyes automatically going to his as the electric current of sensation sizzled along her nerve endings.

'Keep it, if you like, for our next road trip.'

Even a mocking suggestion of a repeat trip with her breasts crushed against his hard back, the male scent of him in her nostrils, sent a shameless rush of liquid heat through her body that pooled between her thighs.

Her little rabbit-jump step back caused her backside to hit the gleaming monster of a sleek designer car behind her and set off the alarm. Wincing at the high-pitched shriek, she pressed her hands to her ears and backed away from the car.

'Do something…' she shouted above the din that bounced and echoed around the cavernous space.

Presumably he did because the noise stopped abruptly and Lizzie's shoulders sagged in relief as she let her hands fall away from her ears.

'Thank God!'

CHAPTER TWO

ADONIS RAISED A hand to acknowledge the two uniformed figures who had appeared from a concealed side door. 'Will you excuse me a moment?' He tossed the words over his shoulder as he strolled decisively towards them.

Lizzie expelled a long sighing breath as her eyes followed his distinctive stride, and she focused with fierce determination on not thinking too much about the finger-in-the-socket electric contact.

Obviously the prohibition had the opposite effect and she relived the moment all over again and again…and what about the disturbing pull she experienced when she came within his orbit?

She needed to be objective and not over-think it, and, in her defence, he possessed an overwhelmingly powerful physical presence, mind-numbing in its strength.

The obvious way to cope with someone like

him was to listen and ignore, so why did she feel compelled to challenge him? It wasn't as if she didn't have experience of alpha men. Her dad was a classic case, and she had learned that keeping quiet and going her own way was the simplest, most pain-free route for both of them to deal with what she privately thought of as his man-child tantrums.

Why wasn't she utilising this tried and tested tactic now? Whenever he delivered one of his pronouncements that always came with the subtext that he was right and not agreeing was not an option, she felt like a cat having its fur brushed the wrong way.

Having ascertained that he now appeared to be deep in conversation with the security guards, she took the opportunity to ring the stables, not just to distract herself, but because they were short-staffed this week due to some sort of bug going around and she felt guilty leaving them in the lurch this way.

The security guards were chatty. It was several moments before Adonis could extract himself from a motor-racing-related conversation—one guard was a fan and had seen him in the VIP area of a race meeting the previous month.

When he did escape he saw the diminutive

figure was looking at her phone, her frown suggesting she had discovered there was no signal down here.

This was confirmed when her crude curse echoed around the space.

Adonis's lips twitched. He was beginning to realise that he had made the mistake of forming a character assessment on one meeting, an awful dress and information sourced from Deb, who had turned out to be not the most scrupulously honest source.

Lizzie was not the mousey, not too bright nepo baby too fragile for life outside her over-privileged little bubble. The alternative was a slightly more subtle version of her cousin.

She fell into neither category. She resembled a mule more than a mouse. She was no Deb lite, she was another species.

Though physically, he conceded as his eyes lingered on her soft profile, the little pointy chin, softly rounded smooth cheeks, she resembled neither a mule nor a mouse.

Obviously she was no great beauty, her features did not have the required regularity, but the combination of the big dramatic blue eyes, fake or not, and the sexy mouth was striking, and her freckle-sprinkled skin had an almost translucent quality.

What she was wearing today was not terrible, but the thigh-length tunic topped by an oversized chunky sweater over badly cut jeans did not shriek style, or a woman who wanted to showcase her femininity.

Strip off a few layers and she might even have a figure, he acknowledged as he walked back to her side, gesturing towards the lift and suggesting once more, 'Shall we take this up to my apartment?'

'No.'

His high-voltage smile faded. He was not accustomed to people who did not fall in with his plans, especially women, and he had put real effort into the smile.

'I'm late,' Lizzie said to soften her abrupt response. 'So if you could just explain the situation and I will be...' She made a fluttering gesture, the action making the loose sleeve of her sweater fall back, revealing a very slim wrist and a scar.

She saw him looking and pulled her sleeve down.

'I'd be grateful if you could, erm...set the record straight, as soon as possible,' she said, aiming for scrupulously polite if a bit distant.

A waste of time. He acted as though she hadn't said anything at all.

'Late for what?' he said, looking her up and down in a way that made her want to wrap her arms around herself or at least add another layer even though the scrutiny was, if anything, impersonal.

Since puberty hit she had suffered a thousand moments of wanting to do that when she had been on the receiving end of crude remarks about her breasts, before she had discovered that layering and baggy and shapeless achieved the desired concealing effect.

'I have told you. Work.'

His dark brows rose towards his darkly defined hairline. 'Wow, you really would be a nightmare interview. Have you signed the Official Secrets Act or what?'

His sarcasm brought colour to her cheeks and ignited wrathful blue fire in her eyes. 'What is it with you? You want to know how the other half lives?'

'Rafe Sinclair's daughter thinks she knows how the other half lives? Give me a break.' Though she might learn sooner than she imagined if she was genuinely ignorant of Sinclair's precarious financial situation.

His dismissive drawl made her fists clench. He really was, she decided, a deeply unpleasant man!

'Actually I volunteer in a stables,' she snapped out, not bothering to describe the non-profit establishment that, alongside an animal rescue, ran classes for disabled children and adults.

'Great stuff, admirable, though I suppose some people might suggest when Daddy is paying your rent you can afford to volunteer.'

'Some people? If you're going to be judgemental and sneery you might as well have the balls to own it!' she snapped back with a sweet, achingly insincere smile that transitioned in the blink of an eye to contempt as she read his expression. He was outraged. How very predictable, she thought, feeling a little glow of superior pleasure. 'And before you start getting all "how very dare you", can't you just tell me what happened back there? Those people? Who fed them that false information?'

How very dare? Adonis was starting to think that this woman would dare pretty much anything! His curiosity was piqued, he had to admit it, that stubborn chin, those glorious lips... Out of nowhere he found himself wondering how hard it would be to hear hoarse gasps of pleasure on them, not contemptuous insults.

'And why,' she continued, wishing she could control her antagonism, actually wishing he were not such an aggravating man, 'did they think that we were a...?' She stopped, unable to finish the sentence. It was just too embarrassing.

He looked more curious than alarmed as he queried, 'Did you say anything to them?'

'About what?'

'Our engagement,' he drawled sarcastically.

Her eyes widened to their fullest extent before squeezing tight closed as she grabbed her head between her hands, her fingers sinking into the rich silky strands of her hair.

Nostrils flared, she sent him a drop-dead glare as she snapped out a resentful reproof. 'I'm glad you can laugh about it.'

'If this came out of the blue for you, I can see it is a difficult situation!'

The concession drew a hoot of laughter from her. 'Of course it came out of the blue,' she snarled, thinking, But not to you.

'But don't pull your hair out.' It was very pretty hair, rich, like glassy silk, with the sort of gloss you rarely saw outside a shampoo advert. Did it feel as silky as it looked?

Her hands fell self-consciously away from her head. 'I'm not. This may seem amusing to you, but it's not to me. None of this has anything to do with me, and I want my life back without people camping on my doorstep. So fix it!' she bellowed.

'Calm down!' he said warily. The last thing he needed was for her to work herself into another asthma attack, but he was also fascinated by the heaving of her breasts against the thick wall of her heavy sweater. 'Apparently an announcement was put in several newspapers today.'

She went pale digesting this information, finding the slow drip-feed of information torturous.

'Saying what?' she snapped back, feeling as if he was playing with her and not much liking it. 'I know you think I'm dim but nice. Actually I am neither.'

He gave a sardonic smile. 'I am not finding you particularly nice.' He was finding her a lot of other things, which he suspected were shading his decision-making to some degree.

For the first time he was taking on board that this woman with an abrasive quotient way out of proportion to her size might not be a person who wanted sympathy, actually hated it, probably hated it almost as much as he did.

'It was an announcement of our engagement placed by our respective families.'

Lizzie had been focused on a point over his

left shoulder. She gave a wild little laugh, her thoughts twirling dizzily, and her horror-filled eyes met his.

'How?' she said, clinging to her denial like someone drowning... This could not be happening, but actually it was the first time any of this made sense. This was a case of mistaken identity. He was engaged and somehow her name had appeared instead of his new fiancée's.

'Oh, I'm so sorry,' she breathed. 'Your fiancée!' She gasped, thinking, If I feel ill at the thought imagine how she must be feeling! The woman he was actually engaged to. 'Well it can be fixed with a retraction and I'm glad you're...' Like he cares about that, Lizzie. 'It's been two years. I'm sure Deb would have wanted you to find someone,' she murmured, falling back on the conventionally polite lie.

In reality Deb had always been very possessive, and if she couldn't have something she had made sure nobody else could have it.

Lizzie was immediately ashamed of the uncharitable thought. Poor Deb was tragically not here to defend herself, and Lizzie was no longer twelve. Though even after all this time, she could still see Deb's look of triumph when she had handed back the princess doll that had been in Lizzie's Christmas stocking, not her own…with its golden tresses hacked off.

A fiancée?

Find someone?

His brow furrowed in bemusement as he struggled to make sense of her sudden change in attitude. She seemed relieved.

'I'm sure she, your fiancée, must be very upset, but it's easy to put right.'

And until then her own life was where exactly?

It would be a story, wouldn't it?

And she would be at the centre of that story?

Her nightmare was being at the centre of anything. Her publishers had been incredibly frustrated when she had refused to do any publicity, but of course in the end the mystery—Who is this woman?—and the ensuing speculation had sold it, which, as her agent had told her, was all that mattered.

Fascinated, he watched the play of emotion across her expressive face. 'I'm not too happy discussing my marriage plans in the open,' he proceeded cautiously.

If he immediately corrected her mistaken belief that this situation was about a misprint, which appeared to be the conclusion she had jumped to, he could see them spending the night in this damned garage with her arguing the odds. 'How about we take this upstairs?'

Take this upstairs...

She brought her lashes down in a protective screen as her wilful imagination lent those words a very different meaning.

She shook her head, willing the guilty fire in her cheeks to cool. 'Is that really necessary?'

'I think so, yes.'

'Oh, all right, then.' She huffed out an eloquent sigh. 'I wish I could start this day all over again.' If she had she would not have got out of bed. While she liked to think she didn't run away from tough situations, burying her head in a duvet held a lot of appeal at that moment.

She flinched at the light touch of his hand on the small of her back and tilted her head upwards. The hand was no longer in contact with her skin but she could feel the warmth, which the logical part of her knew was an illusion. Even so she allowed that warmth to guide her into the lift.

She didn't say a word as the lift swished silently upwards to his apartment, but he decided he preferred her sly digs and outright antagonism to this silence.

He was convinced now that she had not been

party to any of this, unless she was an award-winning actress.

It might not have been his doing, and he was as much a victim of his grandfather's machinations as she was, but he felt a stab of inconvenient guilt anyway. His grandfather wouldn't give a damn about collateral damage so long as he got what he wanted, but her father must have been complicit. He had to be.

The private lift opened directly into the sort of apartment she had imagined someone like Adonis Aetos would call home.

Dizzying high ceilings, pale wooden floors, acres of glass with a view she wasn't interested in, blonde, bland and expensive, she silently decided, her knees folding as she was pushed into a chair.

A glass with something amber in it appeared, and, not looking at the person delivering it, she swallowed it all in one gulp, ignored the burning sensation, and held out her hand mutely for a refill.

After a pause the refill, or at least a small one, arrived, and she disposed of that.

'I don't actually drink spirits,' she mentioned after the fact.

His mobile lips twitched. Strangely she was

the sort of woman who made you want to laugh and hug her at the same time. He'd never been a hugger and he couldn't see any man hugging her without being able to resist the invitation of that lush mouth.

'No, I can see that.'

'I'm quite hot.' She struggled to pull off her outer layer, a heavy Guernsey sweater, before dropping it and subsiding in her seat.

Adonis watched as she folded herself into the chair, the action revealing a gap of bare flesh between the floral tunic that had ridden up dramatically and her jeans, which had slipped down to hip level, the belt appeared to be the only thing holding them up and it was cinched in as tight as it would go. Either she had lost a lot of weight or she habitually wore clothes two sizes too large.

He suspected the latter.

The busily patterned fabric of the tunic pulled tight across centrefold breasts—not that he had personally ever seen a centrefold. Did they even exist any more? The bare area extended from the edge of her ribcage to just below her waist and the section of smooth skin had a pearlescent quality. Her waist was so narrow that he found himself speculating that he could span it with his hands.

Her body, the bits he'd seen, were a total revelation.

The woman hid this body, very successfully, in a world where... He expelled a deep sigh and tore his gaze free. Who knew? barely covered his shock or his... He filtered the thoughts in his head and chose confusion—it was easier to admit to than arousal.

How was this even possible?

The phrase kept playing in his head like the needle on an old-fashioned vinyl record stuck in a groove.

'Sorry, I lost it there for a moment there. Things caught up with me, but I'm totally fine now,' she promised, fixing him with a solemn, slightly glazed, sincere stare. 'Your fiancée, she must be a bit...cross? Tell her I'm sorry, though actually I really haven't done anything, have I? I'm a victim...' The discovery came with a grimace of distaste. 'God, don't you hate being thought of as a victim? I do. I think I might have drunk that...?'

'Brandy.'

She nodded sagely. 'I thought so. Nice. It stings but so does whisky, I think, and I might have swallowed it a bit too quickly. Let's be honest, it was wasted on me. I'm more of a prosecco and soda girl or maybe a white wine

spritzer. Don't touch a cocktail—they are le-
thal, don't you think? There's a lot of snob-
bery about alcohol, I think. You do know...'
she added, noticing the clinging leather she was
sitting in but not his fascinated expression and
thinking, I have to stop talking '...this is a really awful chair, and I bet it cost you a fortune,
but they saw you coming. All style over sub-
stance. I'm really going to stop talking now...
Can I have a coffee? Maybe several.'

'That might be a good idea. I'll organise it.'

He returned a few moments later minus his
leather jacket and carrying a tray with a coffee pot and cups.

'Oh, my...!' she said, staring at his white
tee shirt.

'Is there a problem?'

'Oh, no, you just have... You must work out,'
she said, her eyes fixed on his biceps.

'Upon occasion.'

After several coffees interspersed by a few
intervals when she fought off the impulse to
close her eyes, Lizzie tuned back in.

'Do you have anything to eat—a sandwich
maybe? I'm starving.'

Adonis watched as his visitor—or should
he call her his future wife?—tucked into a
cheese sandwich, the production of which had

exhausted his culinary skills and would have won the scorn of Dmitri, who was due to come back today after a week's downtime.

Dmitri filled his freezer with edible and healthy things. He did a lot of other things that Adonis missed when the older man was absent. After Dmitri had quit his job as Head of Security to help his wife care for their autistic son, Adonis had persuaded him to return and take on a more wide-ranging, flexible remit. There were few people that Adonis trusted implicitly and Dmitri was one of them. Considering the fact that he and Adonis's PA were married, Dmitri already had access to Adonis's diary—the role was almost a job share and the couple had complementary skills.

Initially the older man had been reluctant to accept what he had suspected was a charitable non-role, but he had soon realised after a short trial period that Adonis really did need him.

The line between employer and friend had become invisible. Next week Dmitri was sifting through the candidates for a new member of Adonis's security team, today he was meant to be coming here, officially to discuss the forthcoming trip to California but Adonis knew he would be trying to persuade him to attend his parents' anniversary bash.

He'd fail.

'Sorry, I can't drink,' Lizzie admitted, self-consciously brushing the crumbs off her upper lip. 'But you have to admit… Your poor fiancée. You have to sort this out.'

'I don't have a fiancée.'

She blinked. Her voice, which he had noticed was warm and throaty when she wasn't screeching at him, sounded hoarse as she stammered, 'I—I don't understand. Why…? H-how?'

'The why is fairly simple: my grandfather thinks I need a wife. He decided to…intervene.'

Simple, he said. It didn't sound simple to Lizzie. Aware that she was in danger of hyperventilating, she tried to slow her breathing but it was outside her control. Her sense of confused outrage was escalating, not receding.

'How? Your grandfather did this!'

The heaving bosom, the narrowed, outraged blue stare that fixed on him like a laser—literally nothing could have been farther removed from the angry gaze he remembered at that dismal dinner party. It was focused on hating him in a much more personal way.

'Well, I don't have a signed confession, but his fingerprints are all over it. Do you need your inhaler?'

Her response to his concern was devoid of

any gratitude; instead, there was plenty of exasperation. 'Oh, for heaven's sake, relax. I have been managing my asthma since I was ten years old. I'm fine. Your grandfather, really... that is just a...a wicked thing to do.'

'Possibly...' There was a fractional hesitation before he added, 'But he is dying and I am actually quite fond of the old bastard.'

He gave a bleak smile as his magnificent shoulders lifted in an accepting shrug.

She was totally disarmed, not just by this bombshell, but by this chink in his almost inhuman control. Her glance drifted to the vein beating in his temple as the small crack in her outrage widened before, like ice cream in a microwave, it melted into gloop.

'I'm sorry,' she said awkwardly. 'I didn't know about your grandfather.'

'It is not widely known outside the family and,' he added, his hard stare so obsidian dark it was difficult to believe the glimpse of vulnerability moments earlier had not been an hallucination, 'I would prefer it stayed that way.'

Did he think she was about to blab to the world?

Swallowing her indignation at the implication there was a danger she would not respect his family's privacy, she nodded then hesitated, emotion swelling in her throat as she reminded herself that just because he was far too good-looking and had thought she was pregnant, that didn't make him an evil person. She almost hoped he'd do something awful so she could put him back in that convenient box labelled 'toxic and no redeeming features' in her head.

'I'm sorry, it's hard, I know, when someone you love… I hope…'

Adonis watched her blue eyes fill with tears, the muscles of her throat working as she swallowed before she pinned on a smile and, after a small hesitation, said brightly, 'Do you possibly have a glass of water?'

He arched a brow. 'Brandy?'

Tears still sparkling in her eyes, her husky laugh rang out. The throaty sound made his dark eyes widen. That was a sexy bedroom laugh from somewhere in his subconscious. An image of her shedding another layer and standing, or preferably lying there in her… Realism intervened and he realised there would not be silk and things involved. Never in his imagination or outside it had utilitarian white cotton aroused him more.

Her loud sniff brought him into the moment and out of the rapidly escalating strip-poker fantasy playing out in his head.

'I think I'll pass. Just water, that would be lovely.'

'Water it is. Give me a moment.'

Before he had risen to his feet, a figure appeared wearing an overcoat that his vast shoulders stretched. He stood there, an expectant expression on his craggy features.

'Hi, boss. Water, was it?'

'Impeccable timing as always.' Dark eyes flickered to Lizzie. 'Biscuits?'

She shook her head.

'Sure thing.'

She felt the hooded gaze move over her before he vanished. Obviously it wasn't her place to ask who he was but even when, unexpectedly, Adonis reacted to her unspoken question she was not much the wiser.

'Dmitri is my… He is… Actually he doesn't have a title, but you can trust him.'

'I don't trust you.'

He leaned back in his seat, extending his long legs, and crossed one ankle across the other, the action pulling the faded black denim close across his thighs as he studied her for a long uncomfortable moment before asking, 'Do you always say what you think?'

'Hardly ever.' It must, she decided, be the brandy.

'Then,' he said, executing an elegant mock bow from a sitting position, 'I am honoured.'

Lizzie was alarmed because she felt pleased, as if they were on the same page, which they clearly were not, so she said nothing.

The water arrived, ice clinking on glass delivered on a tray. The character without a title was now in sleeves rolled up to reveal tattooed forearms. 'No biscuits, but there is a cookie mix in the freezer I could…'

'No, I'm fine, thank you.'

She waited until he had gone. 'He cooks.'

'No, but he has a sweet tooth and my housekeeper adores him.'

'Is she here too?' She looked around as though she expected people to materialise from the walls.

'No, here at least I can be alone. Susan does the housekeeping and makes sure I have no sour milk in my fridge. She and Dmitri fill my freezer with meals, unnecessary, because I rarely eat in and delivery from…' he mentioned a Michelin-starred establishment that made her eyes widen '…is simple.'

She wondered whether he actually believed the three-Michelin-starred establishment did takeout, or whether his bubble was so secure that reality never impinged on it.

'Thanks...' She lifted the glass and took a sip, eying him over the rim as she admitted, 'Alcohol at this time of day.' Actually, alcohol at any time of day was an issue for her. 'I might have overreacted. I'm sure you'll sort it and things will go back to normal. Is your grandfather...confused?' she wondered tactfully.

Lizzie knew that people did not always like to discuss dementia and she of all people respected that privacy, the need to protect loved ones from speculation.

'Confused?'

'Your grandfather?' she repeated. An image of a craggy-faced man at the awful dinner, with his blade of a nose and a mop of silver-shot black hair, flashed into her head. She had been introduced and been slightly repelled by his black heavy-lidded stare, not that she had held his attention for more than a moment.

'What makes you say that?'

'Dementia, it can be hard for the family.' And it would totally explain the announcement. 'My mum once left me in a department-store restaurant and went home.'

'How old were you?'

She shrugged. 'Around ten.'

'She must have been very young?'

Lizzie nodded.

'No, my grandfather does not have dementia. Spyros is as sharp as a tack.' And as ruthless as a wolf. 'However, he is dying…cancer.'

The curt delivery was calm, almost cold, but the telltale quiver around his taut jaw suggested that he cared a lot more than he wanted to let on.

'I am sorry…'

People said it, the words were an automatic reflex, but the difference was she meant it. The growing suspicion that it was not an act with her, that it was never an act with her, disturbed him.

He found deceit much easier to manage.

'He's already lived six months longer than they gave him. It is not common knowledge.'

She ignored the second implication that she would blab his personal business to the world.

'He wants me to marry and provide an heir, hence the engagement announcement as a way of forcing my hand.'

This time she allowed the implication that she had no say in the matter to pass because surely it wasn't the only hole in this crazy theory. 'Surely not.'

'Two years ago to the day I was meant to be marrying Deb.' Her stricken look made him grin in what she might once have considered an utterly heartless way, but now she suspected it was all part of hiding his true feelings.

Then again, maybe he didn't have any true feelings to hide.

'I didn't realise.'

'Why would you? Before your earlier shock-horror gasp, I was about to explain that my grandfather let it be known to me at Deb's funeral that six months is an acceptable period of grieving and then you get on with it.'

'He said that?' She studied his face. 'No, not seriously.'

'No one has ever accused my grandfather of possessing a sense of humour.'

'People in pain say things they don't really mean.'

He looked at her, curiosity shining in his hooded eyes. 'Have you always believed everyone has good in them?'

Her chin lifted in response to the mockery in his voice. 'I am not naive or gullible, if that is what you are suggesting. Whatever your grandfather's motivation, he can't think that just because of an announcement in a newspaper you'll marry, even if I would agree, which obviously I don't,' she began a little incoherently, then paused, her blue eyes narrowing. 'Why me?'

'I think it is possible this was a collaborative approach.'

She shook her head. 'What are you talking about?'

'Your father.'

'You are not suggesting…?' She fixed him with a grim glare and slammed her glass down on the table, sending splashes across its surface.

'Your father. Is it Lizzie or Elizabeth or Lizzie Rose?'

She just glared back at him.

'Your father is in a financially compromised situation.'

Choosing to be offended by the suggestion, she shook her head, not wasting words on her response. 'Rubbish!'

'He is within a hair's breadth of going bust, being declared bankrupt.'

She opened her mouth and closed it. He watched her face, a study in stillness, her eyelashes flickering against her smooth cheeks.

CHAPTER THREE

'IS THIS YOUR version of inarticulate rage?'

Lizzie expelled the breath she'd been holding and slung him a killer look. 'That is me thinking,' she snapped, pointing at her face.

He arched a brow. 'I hardly dare ask.' She looked at him blankly. 'What you were thinking,' he elaborated.

'You really don't want to know,' she snapped.

He threw back his head and laughed.

'Even if what you said about Dad is true, and I don't believe you…he would never trade me.'

Studying her set expression, he let it pass, feeling a pang of sympathy for how she was going to feel when she realised the truth. Her parent was willing to use her—a lesson he had learnt early in life.

'I'm willing to hear any alternative theories.'

'I can see your situation is difficult but if you speak to your grandfather I'm sure he will understand everyone grieves in a different way.

Grieving is… There can't be a timetable for such things, and Deb was so very beautiful.'

'Do you still believe in Santa Claus and the Easter Bunny too?' he drawled. 'There is no well of human understanding. My grandfather has always lived by his own rules, and now he has been robbed of that by a disease that doesn't care he is Spyros Aetos. He has no control over the disease, but there are things he still does have control over.'

'You, you mean. Then I feel sorry for you, but my dad would have no part in something so mad, so crazy.'

'Being in financial difficulties makes the crazy seem perfectly legitimate. I do understand his position…the fait accompli is all my grandfather though.'

'My dad doesn't have financial difficulties.'

'Your father has had money problems for some time. He overextended himself after Deb died. He made some reckless moves. Some very ill-judged decisions that could have paid off, but they didn't. He was greedy.' He acknowledged her angry little squeak of protest with a sardonic lift of one dark brow.

'I would know.'

'The banks have refused to give him another extension.'

'What are you saying?' She shook her head, not leaving him space to answer. She knew exactly what he was saying. 'I can't believe that he would not have told me.'

'You can believe it, though, can't you?' he said, studying her face. He had rarely seen anyone who was less able to hide their feelings. 'Of course, you know him better than me.'

'My dad is very proud of what he has achieved.'

'And how do you think he'd react to losing it?'

Her chin lifted at the sly insertion. 'He'd never, never sell me...'

'Well, let's be honest, that is exactly what he is doing. I have some knowledge of your father and he has never struck me as a man who would admit his own failings, especially to a woman, and a woman who is his daughter.

'But he is... A lot of people work for him. What will happen to them?'

'I'm impressed you are thinking about others,' he said, not sounding at all impressed. 'But you've never been poor.'

She flashed him an impatient look. 'I can look after myself.'

'You planning on getting a paid job at the stables? That might involve getting your pretty hands dirty mucking out. Wouldn't you miss your pretty cottage, your allowance?'

Her laugh cut off his taunts and she had the satisfaction of seeing a puzzled expression flicker across his lean face. She had surprised Adonis Aetos, and she was willing to bet that not many people managed that.

'You think you know me, but actually you know nothing about me.'

'Then educate me.'

She hesitated and then shrugged. 'Fine. I don't have an allowance. The cottage is mine.'

He shrugged, assuming that she had received an inheritance from her mother's estate. It didn't really change the essentials. She didn't possess the skill or the will to earn her own living.

'As for getting my hands dirty?' She extended her hands palm upwards and turned them over, displaying her neatly trimmed, short, unpolished nails. 'I have no problem with that, no problem at all.'

She paused, her eyes widening. 'How much money does Dad need, do you think?' she wondered out loud. Her brief flare of hope faded. The investment that she'd only last week signed off on meant that she had no access to her money for four years. Money she had thought she could not possibly need.

'How much do you suppose my cottage is worth?'

Her first instincts appeared to be shockingly selfless. A day-old chick probably had more self-protective instincts than this woman.

'It would not make a dent in what your father owes the bank.'

'There must be some way,' she murmured under her breath.

'There is…' He paused, clicking his tongue as he leaned forwards and removed her white-knuckled hands from the arms of the chair and laid them on her lap.

Her blue eyes flew to his face.

'You'll cut off the circulation,' he said, unable to take his eyes off the specks of blood on her full lower lip where she had worriedly gnawed at the soft flesh. She had a mouth that fantasies were made of.

'Don't worry. I think your father has found his own way—'

'You can't say that,' she tossed back angrily. 'This is guesswork. You're just—'

'Not exactly,' he interrupted. 'I have an inside source in my grandfather's office who—'

She launched to her feet. 'Spies for you! That's disgusting. You spy on your own family!'

'I do not spy on my family,' he contradicted,

looking irritated by her emotional response. 'I have someone close to my grandfather who has his best interests at heart. He did not reveal any secrets, but when I suggested a hypothetical scenario that involved your father pocketing cash and us walking dutifully up the aisle he did not deny it.'

'That sounds like spying to me,' she countered, clinging to her denial as she started restlessly pacing the room, pausing to finger a lamp or stroke a cold marble surface tinged to a warm glow by the sun shining through the tinted plate-glass wall.

He watched her, able to feel the tension emanating from her as he got to his feet in one lithe motion. 'So you accept we have been set up.'

She paused and turned. Her height advantage had only ever been an illusion and as he uncoiled to his full height with lazy elegance she recognised it as such.

She nodded, pressing a hand to her forehead as the words filled with pent-up emotion burst from her. 'I know I'm not the son, or even the daughter, especially the daughter, he wanted, but how…how could Dad have put me in this position?'

'Desperation makes men do reckless things.'

'Crazy things!' she contradicted.

'Semantics and your moral outrage aside, you say this is a crazy action?' He shrugged. 'And yes, but it is fuelled by desperation. Will you listen for a moment?' he snapped, cutting off her imminent protest and grabbing both her wrists before she could continue her agitated pacing.

He loomed over her, capturing her eyes with his.

'Will you listen?'

After a moment she nodded, mainly because she couldn't escape his dark stare.

'My grandfather knew about the seriousness of his condition for six months before he informed anyone in the family, which was when I approached someone who is loyal to him.'

'Your spy?'

'He agreed to inform me if there were things pertaining to his health that I...we as a family needed to know. Last month he was given the news that he only had weeks to live.'

The muscles quivering along his taut jaw gave a lie to his emotionless delivery. Despite the situation, Lizzie's tender heart ached for him, though she was aware he was not interested in her heart, tender or otherwise.

He cleared his throat. 'The latest scans show there are more secondary tumours, this time in his brain.'

'Your family—'

'This is not news I have shared except with you. My father would have him declared unfit if he got wind of it. They have never…got on.'

'You think this explains…' she spread her hands wide and shook her head '…this…today.'

'Who knows?' He held her eyes in a stranglehold grip, the message in his dark-lashed compelling stare grave and sombre. 'I'd like my grandfather to die a happy man.'

She didn't pretend not to understand what he was saying.

'Would you being engaged…? Would it really make that much of a difference to him?'

'Me being married, the idea that I would produce the heir he longs for, but I think it wise to keep a closer eye on things, which is why I was making arrangements to go home, but events have moved on. Now I think the best way to deal with this is… Well, cut out the middleman.'

'How do you mean?'

'I'm sure that the matchmakers have their next move planned. Your father will appeal to your better nature. You clearly have one,' he observed, making it sound like a flaw. 'My grandfather will… Well, let's face it, he has the winning hand. He is dying.'

'Not really a winning hand… Sorry, I didn't mean to be flippant.'

'You're just being factual, but I'm assuming you get my drift?' he said, as though it was obvious.

'Not really.'

'I think we should get married!'

CHAPTER FOUR

'YOU ARE CERTIFIABLE!' Lizzie said with deep conviction.

'The fact is your father does have a financial black hole that my grandfather is willing to plug if he persuades you of the advantages of marrying me. The engagement was apparently the first act, meant, I assume, to set the ball rolling.' He dropped languidly into a seat. 'It would be easy for us to call their bluff, but, as I say, I'm fond of my grandfather. Where's the harm?'

His casual offhand question made her leap out of her seat. The sight of him sprawling there looking so relaxed sent her temper soaring.

'Are you off your head? Harm. Harm!' she spat out, stabbing the air with a finger before pointing it at him. 'You know what I think? I think you are deranged! I think this is all some

fantasy you have created. Well, I'm not buy-
ing into it.'

'A fantasy where I need to blackmail you
into marriage?'

His sarcasm brought an angry flush to her
cheeks.

'There is an easy way to settle this one way
or the other. Call your father. Ask him.'

She blinked, taken off balance by his suggestion. 'Call him?'

He nodded. 'Why not? Unless you are scared
of the answer you get.'

Her chin went up. 'I'm not scared,' she lied.

'Fine. I'll give you the room.'

He returned twenty minutes later to find Lizzie
still pacing the room. She paused when she saw
him. He studied her face for a moment and experienced a rare stab of compassion—her expression told him everything he needed to know.

'I've spoken to Dad.'

He watched her gather herself and didn't
push. It was not a leap to assume she hadn't
liked what she had heard.

'I always thought that he was confident but
really…he's—' She couldn't bring herself to
say weak. She loved her dad and she always
would.

'The man is in financial trouble. He's desperate and he's proud,' Adonis said.

The defence coming from the most unlikely source made her shake her head. Amazingly, Adonis Aetos was showing more compassion than she felt able to at that moment.

'Proud, yes, he is, and he's self-entitled.' Shocked by the audible bitterness in her voice, she put her hand to her mouth. Snippets of their recent conversation flying piecemeal into her head. Her dad had gone from denial to anger, to pleading.

'He didn't say sorry. Nothing was his fault.'

Had it ever been?

An image of him sitting on the sofa, his head in his hands, when the doctor had explained that Lizzie would always have a scar after the scalding incident.

'You should have stopped her,' her dad had yelled. 'You should have come and got me. This wouldn't have happened if you had watched her.'

Lizzie, shamed, had said, 'Yes, Dad.' Even though he hadn't been there to get—he rarely had been during the latter stages of her mum's disease—and Lizzie had been watching her. She had only gone outside for a few minutes to play with the new kitten. Mum's carer—by that point she had needed full-time care—had been upstairs turning off the bath tap before it overflowed again.

When Lizzie had come back in, her mum, wearing a glittery and saturated evening dress, had been in the kitchen and there had been a full pan of boiling water bubbling furiously on the stove.

Lizzie had got between her mum and the pan but when Lizzie had stretched up to switch the gas ring off, her mum had made a grab for the pan.

Most of the boiling water had spilled harmlessly on the floor, except for the amount that had hit Lizzie's wrist before she'd jumped back. The scarring would have been worse if the carer hadn't returned and immediately plunged Lizzie's arm under cold running water.

'Your father needs validation and approval. He can't admit a weakness or own a mistake.'

She blinked, her lashes fluttering against her cheek at this objective and painfully accurate assessment.

'Do you think people change?' she wondered.

'No.'

She nodded, then said defensively, 'I love

him,' before adding, 'You love your grandfather and he's not perfect!'

'Unlike you, this comes as no great shock to me and I have always found perfection a dead bore. Did you tell your father you would save him?'

'No.'

'Only human to want him to stew for a while.'

She gasped. There were just so many things wrong with that statement. 'I do not want revenge on my dad and you are speaking as though I have already agreed.'

'Your father thinks you will. He is relying on it.'

She gave a bitter little laugh and addressed his claim with weary resignation. 'He thinks I'm a pushover and so do you!'

'Maybe you're just too lazy to push back?'

'Do I come across as someone who cares what you think about me?' she flared.

'I think you sell yourself short, which is entirely up to you,' he drawled. 'No judgement. Your father, on the other hand, needs the world's approval. He sees himself through the eyes of others and yes, actually, plenty of judgement there.'

Not you, she thought, staring up at the tall alpha male figure. On many levels he remained an enigma to her. Superficially he and her dad were two generations of the stereotypical alpha male. But her dad was playing a part. His confidence was a thin veneer hiding his inadequacies. Adonis's was not an act, was not a veneer of confidence. It was at a cellular level. She was betting he had never needed anyone's approval in his life. His confidence was not based on how he was perceived by the world. It came from an inner certainty.

He waited, watching the emotions she wore so close to the surface running across her expressive little face.

'You were right… I was wrong about Dad. I am sure he's ashamed deep down. He…he… I think he was crying.' She took a deep breath, the emotional exhaustion she was determined to hide creeping into the tremor in her voice.

Her hunched shoulders, the bruised hurt in her blue eyes, dragged a surge of something he chose not to recognise as protectiveness.

She straightened her shoulders. 'So how would this work?'

'My family, including my grandfather, are at present at the island. It belongs to our family, totally private. There would be no press intrusion for you to deal with for the weeks or months.'

'So the plan would be?'

'We marry, go there and play the newly-weds until the charade is no longer necessary.'

'You make it sound simple. You can't just get married. There is paperwork?' she persisted, hopeful of a flaw in his reasonable-sounding plan.

Reasonable? At what point did insane become reasonable?

She supposed it depended on how it was sold, and Adonis was a very good salesman.

'It is not simple,' he agreed. 'But you don't need to worry about it. I will sort the details.'

'You're relentless, aren't you?'

'I prefer focused.'

'I don't like being organised.'

His lips quirked. 'Yes, I am getting that.'

'So if I agree, in three months' time I'll be married and separated.'

'I thought you already had agreed.'

'That's because you only hear what you want to.'

He laughed then, adopting a more serious note, added, 'Divorce is not a stigma any longer.'

'It's not divorce. It's marriage. It's something I always vowed… I never intended to get married ever.'

His brows lifted at her vehemence, then he watched as the frown lines in her forehead smoothed.

'But this wouldn't count, would it?'

'Legally it will, but, well, obviously it is a transactional arrangement.' Head tilted to one side, he considered her face. He was still adjusting to the fact that he was attracted to her. The more he looked at her face, the more he enjoyed looking. The glimpse of the suggestion of the body underneath the awful clothes had tweaked his interest. Perhaps this was a perversity in the male of the species, the hidden more erotic than flaunting acres of flesh.

Next he'd be getting turned on by a nicely turned ankle.

'Or are you talking about sex?' he said, thinking about it as his eyes sank to the curves she tried hard to conceal.

Her little gasp sounded very loud in the silence that followed.

'No, I am not!' she cried, making a red-cheeked recovery. Angry as much with herself for reacting to his taunting when she was sure he had barely noticed she was a female. 'It had not even occurred to me!' she said with lofty disdain.

'Well, it had occurred to me.'

Lofty disdain vanished as her jaw dropped literally.

He had said it so casually, she would have assumed that he was winding her up if it hadn't been for the gleam she glimpsed in his dark eyes before his heavy lids half lowered.

Imaginary gleam or for-real gleam, the fact that the man frequently billed as the sexiest man on the planet had just said that he had thought about sex with her... Lizzie worked very hard at keeping her face blank, but her defence mechanism failed her, probably due to the fact her hormones were going crazy.

Get a grip, Lizzie, she told herself. *This is a wind-up.*

His dark eyes crinkled at the corners as his head tilted to one side in what she was recognising as a characteristic gesture. He slanted her a curious stare. 'You look shocked.'

The mild surprise in his voice made her want to hit him.

'Just stop! We both know that you already have me, so you can save yourself the bother of resorting to the tired old seduction routine.'

'Tired? I'm offended,' he mocked, his eyes shining with amusement and something else she tried hard not to see.

'If I agree to this, there won't be any sex. I

assumed that was a given,' she said, recalling the occasion when Deb had offered Lizzie her leftover lovers until Lizzie had realised that showing her visceral distaste only encouraged her cousin, who had taken great delight in mocking what she'd seen as Lizzie's prudery.

'A given?' He allowed himself the painful indulgence of wondering about her glowing skin. Was it that smooth and pale all over? Did the freckles extend beyond her pretty nose? 'I think you have not thought this through. We could be together for weeks.'

'I thought that was the idea, me not thinking it through,' she countered, her spiky interruption drawing an unwilling grin from him. 'You rush me into saying yes before I can think about it. And I think I'll be able to last a few weeks without sex.'

He threw back his head and laughed, a warm and uninhibited sound that delivered an extra tingle to her already thrumming body. 'What if I can't?'

Impelled by desperation rather than inspiration, she heard herself blurt out defensively, 'Have you even looked at another woman since Deb?'

Any hint of humour faded from his face—effectively it became an austere, beautiful blank.

A blank that hid a world of pain, she realised, her tender heart aching for him as guilt bit deep.

'Sorry, I didn't mean to… That was a callous thing to say,' she admitted in a small guilt-laden voice.

'I do not want to discuss Deb.'

'No…no, obviously, of course not and neither do I. I knew you were not being serious, I just…' She paused, relieved when he cut across her.

'Histrionics aside, my grandfather is ill, not stupid. To convince him, we are going to have to display some…affection, if we are to sell this to him.'

'He won't expect us to be overcome with lust and have sex on the dining table, will he? Or is that a quaint Greek custom like smashing plates?' The smart words came back to bite her before she had stopped talking.

It was ultra hard to maintain an expression of amused indifference when her wilful imagination supplied the visualisation of the torrid scene she had just described. A gleam in his eye and a few provocative words and she had become a bundle of raging hormones.

God, what was happening to her?

That, she told herself, was a question for

later. Right now her priority had to be concealing the fact. She needed to focus and take control of her rioting hormones.

'My family has its moments but on the whole they are conservative…mostly. Tabletop sex is optional and conducted in private.'

'Have you…?' she began, able to still her tongue by biting it hard, but not the images playing in her head.

The raw lust that was sliding through his body made it hard for Adonis not to react to the open goal she had gifted him. He focused instead on managing the lust, which he assumed had something to do with the drought of late in his sex life.

It wasn't grief or guilt that got in the way of him moving on, it was distrust in his own judgment and boredom. Strange that it took a woman who made no attempt to please him, made no attempt to seduce him, to jolt his libido into full sinful life.

Maybe he needed a challenge, he needed surprises?

She definitely surprised him, though for such a self-possessed female she also had a vulnerability that made him step back when every instinct made him want to move in.

'The point is we are going to be living for a

short period in close proximity.' He paused to allow this fact to register and, from her worried expression, it did. 'For some weeks, possibly months. We will have to act as though we are intimate even if we are not.'

'Months!' The moment the exclamation left her lips she was regretting it. 'Not that I'm wishing your grandfather—'

'I know exactly what you mean.'

'Look, bottom line,' she began awkwardly. Given the circumstances it felt right to explain. 'I am not a very sexual person.' Despite her best intentions, she couldn't hold his gaze when she made this big reveal.

She really believed what she was saying. What or who the hell was responsible for that? he asked himself, feeling contemptuous for a man who had left her feeling lacking. One of those pathetic losers, he speculated, who covered their own failings by saying 'It's not me, it's you'?

'So it is a non-issue. You're safe. There will be no embarrassing incidents. I won't be pushing any... This is not an issue for me.'

'I am difficult to embarrass.'

'That I can believe,' she said with feeling and a wild little laugh. 'But, seriously, I am not going to misinterpret acting for anything else, if that is concerning you. What goes on behind closed doors can be boring.'

He was gripped by a strong conviction that this woman could never be boring.

'You know, I've had a great idea,' she said, her eyes sparking enthusiasm. She placed her hands on the arms of the chair he was sitting in and leaned forward as she lowered her voice to explain. 'You thought I was pregnant when you saw me. Why don't we let people think…? Not lie,' she added swiftly. 'Just more don't deny it if people assume… It would at least give some sort of reason for you to marry me.'

'You mean people will believe you lured me into your bed when I was drunk and incapable and—' He watched her enthusiastic smile become a horrified frozen grimace.

She registered she was standing too close. She also recognised there was a strange reluctance in her to rectify the situation.

'You're right,' she agreed with a sigh.

'I am?' he said cautiously. The scent coming from her warm body, or maybe the hair that hung around her face, was distracting… addictive.

'It was a stupid idea. Your family will look at me and know I am not capable of being sexy and seductive.'

'My family…' he began.

'What?' she prompted, struggling to interpret the odd, almost driven expression on his face.

She was too surprised to react when, without warning, he took her face between his hands and, pulling her down towards him, covered her mouth with his cool lips. She gave herself over to the slow sexual seduction and let everything else vanish… For a few blissful moments it was just texture, heartbeat, taste, tactile, sensual and outside her experience.

Lizzie had been kissed, she had actually enjoyed kisses when her brain could detach from what was happening and explain it away, but this was different, very different.

His lips, the way they moved with slow seductive skill across her mouth, the dip of his tongue and the wild need to meet it, the need to explore and taste were new, scary and exciting territory.

Then it was over and after a moment of deep breaths and eye-clashes she straightened up and took a hasty step back.

'Well, that was—' Probably the most erotic experience of her life, which she supposed made her a sad case.

'Nice?'

His smug mockery stung. If he thought she would say he'd rocked her world he was going to be disappointed, even if it was true.

'Passable.' God, he was so up himself and she was so… Well, actually not being too dramatic, she was doomed.

Every detail was indelibly imprinted into her memory. Every tiny detail recorded, the texture and strength of those long fingers framing her face, the addictive lemony spice scent of his soap. Soap—it sounded so prosaic but so wasn't.

She'd thought she had been kissed before but now she knew she hadn't—not really.

And that mind-expanding, physically debilitating kiss, which meant nothing more to him than, well, shutting her up or proving that he was irresistible. Either option was unpalatable and he'd succeeded on both grounds.

She took a second step backwards when he rose to his feet in one supple fluid motion. She told herself for a split second that she was in control and gave up the exercise of denial because she really wasn't.

It was chemical!

It was insane!

As he watched her Adonis was aware of the predatory pulse inside him. It was attuned to every minute shift of expression on her face. He could almost feel the pulse beating under her skin… He could smell her arousal.

It was basic, primal.

It was all so out of his comfort zone, and then some. When was the last time he had struggled to get his libido in check or needed the effort it now cost him?

He wanted to peel away the layers, quite literally, and discover what this woman had that bypassed every logic circle in his brain.

Was this how his parents functioned—all instinct and no brain, no logic…animalistic?

The thought sent a warning kick to his belly. The chilling idea that he had wandered into his parents' world enabled him to shrug it off. A kiss, as they said, was just a kiss, and she did have that mouth.

So he cut himself some slack.

'You really don't have to worry. I know where we stand and I think we can hold hands and I can laugh at your jokes without being overcome by wild animal passion. I agree it is good to think ahead, but…' She took a deep breath. 'I am not one of your—your groupies, so please remember that in the next weeks.'

'So no more kissing.'

'It's a matter of context, I suppose, and I'm

fine with that,' she lied glibly. 'Deb was...' She paused. 'I know,' she continued gently. 'Gosh, she was a hard act to follow but one day... Sorry,' she added, knowing she had strayed into areas with massive no-go signs. Obviously he was still in love with Deb. She didn't have to labour the point.

His expression did not suggest that he appreciated her delicate negotiation of a difficult subject at all.

'Will there be a prenup?' she said, immediately feeling foolish for querying the obvious. It was normal for a man like Adonis to protect his interests, and that went double when the marriage in question was less one of convenience, more mutual inconvenience, a few weeks or months out of his life to enable his grandfather to die a happy man.

Whether his grandfather deserved this sacrifice was not the issue for Lizzie. She had been a child and helpless to do anything but, when her mum had been dying, she would have broken every rule in the book to make her mum smile...just for a moment.

She wasn't judging him, but she didn't forget that he was not a child, he was a powerful and ruthless man.

'Well, more a post-nup. You will not lose out financially by this.'

She froze. 'I don't want your money. I earn my own money.'

'I thought you volunteered at these stables?'

His patronising undertone set her teeth on edge. 'Felly Edge. Yes, I did work there when I left school, but now I write.'

'Have you had anything published?'

She nodded, telling herself that boasting was a bad thing, although wafting her last royalty statement under his nose at that moment would have given her a lot of satisfaction.

'It is hard to make a living as a writer.'

'I know.' She gritted her teeth, for the first time understanding a little of her team's frustration as she was forced to bite back the literally amazing number of books her series had sold.

Something about him released the dormant boastful voice in her that wanted to be released, that wanted to scream, *Forget about self-deprecating. I have sold a shedload of books. I have earned the praise, the kudos.*

Even if I still feel a fraud.

'What sort of books?'

'Romance.'

'Ahh…' The way he said it made her teeth ache but that might have been the clenching.

'So you are a romantic?'

'Not at all. If you think I am looking for love you could not be more wrong.'

'So you are not looking for love and marriage.'

'There are lots of kinds of love, but it's not love I have an issue with, just the blind belief that love will make everything OK.'

Buried memories aside, she knew that her dad had loved her mum, but he hadn't been able to protect her. Marriage was a formula for…well, not happiness anyway.

'Not really relevant, is it, in this instance?'

At the shrill sound of his phone he pulled it out of his pocket and glanced at the screen. 'Excuse me. I need to take this.'

Left alone, Lizzie began to pace the room.

What had she done?

What had she agreed to?

CHAPTER FIVE

'WHAT ARE YOU DOING?'

Lizzie waited until she had pulled her sweater over her head. 'I'm going home.'

'You can't go back to your cottage. I will arrange for someone to close things up for you and collect your documents. If you are thinking clothes, you will need a new wardrobe anyway so—'

'What is wrong with the clothes I have?'

His eyes moved in a disparaging sweep from her feet to her face. 'Do you really want me to answer that?'

She flushed. 'I won't let you dress me.'

A disturbing smile played across his sensual lips as he studied her. Despite the smile and the mockery in his dark eyes, she sensed a tension about him as he gave his throaty response. 'Husbands are normally more concerned with undressing their wives.' He paused and laughed. 'You blush like a virgin.'

What would he say if she said she was?

She moistened her lips and decided not to find out.

'Do not look at me like that.'

She blinked in bewilderment.

'You are entering into this of your own free will.'

'I know that. Don't flatter yourself that you could force me to do anything.'

'I promise you I have never forced a woman.'

The male arrogance made her laugh. 'No, you just overwhelm them with your wit and charm. Course, you're rich, but I'm sure that has nothing to do with it.'

After a moment's shocked silence he laughed. 'You really don't take prisoners, do you?'

'I didn't mean Deb,' she blurted.

He arched a brow. 'Didn't you?' To her relief he left no gap for her to respond before adding, 'The fact remains you can't go back to your cottage. The press are camped out.'

'How do you know?'

'Why risk it? I think it would be best for you to stay here.'

She laughed. 'That is not happening. I have a cat, which will need feeding when I have or-ganised—'

'You can't stay in your cottage. You will be a target for—'

'I'm not going to stay there. I'll go home. The estate has good security and high walls.'

'So you have a cat, I do not see the relevance. Someone can deal with your cat and have him housed.'

'Mouse is—'

'Mouse? I thought you said you had a cat.'

'I do have a cat. Her name is Mouse. If I'm going to put my life in storage there is no way in the world I am going to allow some stranger to walk into my house and literally pack my life away.'

'Very well, but you will not leave here until it is dark.'

'That's ridiculous!'

'That's the deal and, if it makes you feel any better, I will not be here. Dmitri will see you safely home and then take you to your father's estate.'

'I'll drive myself.'

He clenched his teeth over a robust retort. 'Won't it be awkward for you to see your father just now? What did he say when you said you were coming?' It really didn't seem the best plan to him or, for that matter, any plan at all.

He studied her face. 'You didn't tell him you were coming.'

'He won't be there.'

He arched a brow. 'You know this how?'

'I know my father. Look, it's my home but he really won't be there. Dad always vanishes when there is something he doesn't want to think about.'

'Vanishes?'

'Well, not vanish, more removes himself. When Mum died he went on a six-month cruise.'

The expression on Adonis's lean face made Lizzie regret the confidence.

'He took you with him? How old were you?'

'I was twelve and, no, he didn't take me with him. He couldn't cope with me crying. He sent me postcards though.' A smile played across her mobile mouth as she thought of them lined up around her dressing-table mirror.

Adonis had never been much impressed by Deb's uncle on the occasions they had met, but this artless confidence made any ambivalence vanish. What a loser!

'If you have things to do...?' she said pointedly.

'And deprive you of my company?' he taunted. 'Actually, now is as good a time as any to put things in motion.'

She shook her head. 'What things?'

'A marriage doesn't arrange itself.'

'Oh, I suppose not.'

'I'll keep you up-to-date with the arrangements.'

'Don't bother, I don't need to know the details.' It wasn't as if knowing would make any difference. 'Just do it.'

Lizzie's furtive return to her own home under the cover of darkness made her feel like some sort of thief, even if it was one with a key.

'Was it really necessary to go round the block three times?' she asked Dmitri as they drew up, and immediately felt guilty for the sarcasm because she had no doubt that he was following orders. 'Well, you can tell him there were no ninja warriors hiding in the bushes.'

'I think the odd pap is what worries him most.'

'Well, thanks, I can take it from here.'

She let herself in and, walking to the window to close the blinds, she saw the four-wheel drive still sitting outside. No doubt he'd been told how long to wait—maybe all night? She was considering going outside to inform him when the car drew away, making her glad she hadn't made a fool of herself.

* * *

Dmitri parked up and took out his phone again, ensuring he wasn't driving before he spoke. 'Hi, boss,' he said, settling back into his seat. 'The place was clear, no sign of any journalists, and she's safe inside. I've parked at the end of the street, got a good view of access.'

'Thanks for this,' Adonis said. 'Let me know what time she starts out.'

'You want me to follow her?'

'No, I'll arrange for someone to wait for her to arrive then we can stand down. The Sinclair place apparently has pretty good security.'

Six a.m., the text had said, and the rat-a-tat knock at the door came exactly at six.

Lizzie fought against the tempting idea of ignoring the summons, turning the lock and whisking away upstairs. Maybe there was more of her dad in her than she had thought.

Her prediction that he would have absented himself—his usual way of dealing with un-pleasantness—had been proved right. After his initial message to say he was playing golf in Portugal there had been radio silence.

Last night had been the first night in her own bed for a week, and maybe the last for a long time. The knowledge made her tummy muscles tighten.

After the second knock Lizzie unclenched her fingers one by one and took a deep breath. She tried out several versions of a cool and collected smile in the mirror and settled on a scowl, which came naturally, as she side-stepped the pile of luggage crammed in the small hallway. It was not the set of designer luggage that had been delivered along with a wardrobe of designer clothes brought by a duo who appeared to have been waiting for her return in a van bearing the name of an expensive department store.

Most of the contents of the glossy bags, wrapped between tissue paper or on hangers, were now in the motley collection of her own mismatched bags and holdalls.

True, it was a pretty feeble sort of rebellion, but it went a small way towards making her feel she was in charge of something and not some puppet. Feeble or not, it seemed a principle worth holding onto, and lessened the gut instinct that told her she was being managed.

Heart thudding, she pulled the door open a lot more violently than she had intended. She immediately lowered her line of vision a good four inches—the man standing on her doorstep was not six three. The anticlimax was intense.

'Hello, Miss Sinclair.'

'Hello again, Dmitri,' she said, responding to the greeting in an overly bright voice. 'Does my carriage await?' she asked. Her gaze moved beyond him to the massive four-wheel drive with blacked-out windows parked outside her gate just as the passenger door opened and a woman with short bleached hair spiked around her head appeared.

'My wife, Jenna. We're the witnesses.'

'Oh, that's…good. Well. So, no bridegroom?'

'He's meeting us there.'

She didn't bother asking where there was. It seemed a bit late to take any interest in the details at this stage.

As the broad-shouldered figure picked up several of her bags she grabbed a rucksack and slung it over one shoulder.

'I'll take that,' he protested.

Lizzie ignored him and picked up Mouse, who was looking through the screen of her carrier with an expression of fastidious disgust.

'A cat?' He looked nonplussed.

'Yes, this is Mouse. She's a very good traveller,' she explained, deciding to eliminate all the potential objections straight off. 'And she's got a passport and is up to date with all her jabs.' She strode down the path to the car, not waiting for a response.

'Hi, I'm Jenna.' The openly curious woman looked her up and down. Lizzie assumed the brightly coloured kaftan-style maxi she was wearing was not normal office wear, unless Adonis kept a very informal office, which, considering his sharp suits, did not seem likely.

To Lizzie's annoyance she heard herself say, 'I've got shoes in the bag,' when the other woman reached her seen-better-days trainers.

'Good-looking cat. Do you want to sit up front?'

'No, we're fine in the back,' Lizzie said, warming towards the woman who had admired her cat. 'Oh, the key...' she added, glancing at the baggage-laden figure striding down the path. She put Mouse in the back seat and reached into the front pocket of the rucksack. She was afraid that if she went back into the house she might go inside and lock the door to shut out this insanity.

She was on her way to her own wedding!

'You'll need these,' she said, throwing them to Dmitri, who had finished putting the first load of bags in the boot and was going back for more.

He caught them casually one-handed and nodded.

He made short work of the rest of her bags and Lizzie watched him lock her door. The mundane action seemed scarily symbolic.

It was still home, she reminded herself as she accepted the keys and put them in her bag. When this was over she would be able to walk back into her old life, or reclaim a new life where her dad was not in danger of going under.

She couldn't allow herself to regret her choice. Some people could rebuild their lives after everything went pear-shaped—they could come back bigger and stronger. But her dad was not one of that number. The humiliation of bankruptcy was not something her dad would ever recover from.

'All set back there?'

Lizzie nodded, then realised that no one could see her.

'Yes,' she lied.

'Have you ever been to Gibraltar before?'

'Gibraltar?'

Straining in her seat belt, the older woman twisted around the side of her seat to look at Lizzie. 'Honest to God!' she exclaimed indignantly. 'I made up an information pack for you.

Didn't he give it to you? Typical!' she brooded waspishly.

'Information pack?' Lizzie echoed, thinking, *Oh, be still my beating heart...how romantic!* 'Aren't we going to a register office on the way to the airport?'

'Airport first then wedding. Adonis has been in Gibraltar setting things up for the past few days. It's less complicated to get married at short notice there as a tourist. Didn't he mention that when he rang?'

'He didn't ring, but then,' she added with a bright smile, 'he didn't need to. We hardly chat for hours every night, and I'm not counting the hours until I hear his voice.'

Lizzie stopped abruptly, discomfort spreading in her chest as she tried to read the expression on the other woman's face.

In her desire to make it crystal clear she was not blinded by his smile or besotted by his sexual charisma, she had gone too far. She had also spoken out on the assumption that this couple knew everything, but was this the case? She fretted, her anxiety communicating itself to the cat, who began to miaow loudly.

Jenna also seemed to pick up on Lizzie's unease. 'Don't worry, we both know what's happening,' she said, sounding sympathetic. 'Well, obviously as much as we need to know.'

Probably they know more than I do…

Lizzie felt a stab of resentment. She might have basically said just do it, but that had been a figure of speech. She hadn't meant she wanted to be left in the dark about basic stuff. Adonis was clearly a man who had no problem taking control without any encouragement, and she had encouraged him.

'Can I call you Lizzie? Or do you prefer Elizabeth?'

'Lizzie.' She forced a smile. The other woman seemed friendly and it wasn't her fault. She was obviously just the messenger.

'Do you want to drop the cat off somewhere?' Adonis's PA asked as she pulled back into the front seat.

'No, she's coming with me.'

'She's got a passport,' Dmitri supplied in a voice devoid of all intonation.

'Is that even a thing?' his wife asked doubtfully.

'Yes, it is.'

Lizzie saw the couple exchange glances and her chin locked in stubborn determination. There was no way she was leaving her cat behind.

This was non-negotiable.

Lizzie had not acquired a cat. The cat, a bedraggled, underweight creature when she had arrived, dragging one injured leg behind her, had chosen Lizzie.

No Mouse and there might never have been any bestselling books. She had modelled her feline heroine on the stray who had worked her way into Lizzie's heart.

It was a short flight and, though her dad did not own his own private jet or a fleet of them like the Aetos family, he hired them. It was his preferred form of travel, and Lizzie, who had flown in private jets before, was not overawed, and she wasn't a nervous flyer.

Lizzie had worried a little about how Mouse would adapt. The two times she had taken her cat abroad before it had been by car and ferry, and with the help of a mild sedative—luckily she had had some left over from the last trip, but had not so far administered it. To this point the cat had taken it in her stride.

Released from her carrier once they had taken off, much to Jenna's alarm, the feline had actually enjoyed the attention from the crew, who had fussed over her during the short flight.

Lizzie was not a newbie when it came to flying, but she sat with her nose virtually pressed to the window as they came in over the sparkling waters of the bay, the Rock behind them, and landed on the runway.

It was stunning.

'Incredibly short runway,' Dmitri, who was sitting on the opposite side of the plane, supplied.

'Totally incredible,' Lizzie breathed. 'I felt as though we were going to end up in the sea!'

'Shut up, both of you. You are not, either of you, normal. It is horrific,' Jenna had declared, grabbing her husband's hand in a death grip as they hit the tarmac with a jolt that drew a scream from her.

'Jenna is not a good flyer.'

'I hate you,' his wife said firmly. 'Both of you.'

Lizzie, laughing, unfastened her belt and discovered that the cat, who was safely secured back in her carrier for the landing, was asleep.

'So what happens now?' Lizzie asked, thinking, That was the fun bit, now comes the nightmare. *Man up, woman*, she snapped out in her head.

'Jenna usually throws up.'

Lizzie laughed. She might not like her future

husband, but the people who worked for him were another matter. Unbuckled, she stood up and smoothed the silk of her short blue skirt while Jenna talked her through the immediate schedule displaying brisk efficiency and no visible signs of nausea.

'Through Customs, shouldn't be an issue. Adonis will be meeting us. Nowhere is far from the airport on the Rock. If you want to freshen up or change, Adonis has been using the owner's suite at—'

'He owns a hotel?'

'He does, several actually—he believes in diversification. But the one here belongs to a friend of his.'

Friend covered a lot of territory. Were they talking friend or was it shorthand for old or maybe even present lover?

She pushed the intrusive thought away. Those were not the sorts of questions that came as part of the territory of temporary fake wife.

'But if you don't need to stop, it's straight to the wedding venue, a celebrant and a private setting, for the ceremony. Then it's back here and you fly direct to Xania. You'll be on the island for dinner.' Seeing the expression on Lizzie's stunned face, she paused, seeming to realise she was delivering a lot of information.

'Are you OK?'

'Finding it a bit hard to process,' Lizzie admitted. 'So we are travelling directly to Greece.'

'It isn't a long flight.'

'Then transfer to the island?'

'We can fly direct. It's a recent addition and more an airstrip than airport. Previously you did have to land on the mainland and get a helicopter transfer to Xania, which was a nightmare.'

'Have you stayed at the island much?' She had read up on the Aetos family's private island and seen the photos. 'Island paradise' was an overworked term, but in this instance, if the photos told half the truth, the description was deserved.

'A few times. Not at the house. We stay in one of the bungalows.' Jenna flashed her husband a secret smile. 'It's one with all the facilities we need for Robert when he comes. He just loves it there.'

'Robert?'

'Our son, well, my son. He has some complex needs, but he is spending this week in respite care. He loves it at the farm. He goes there several times a year. We are so grateful to Adonis; the breaks help us.' Lizzie watched the other woman's eyes fill with tears before, after a short struggle, she regained her composure. 'Though of course he says he is the beneficiary of us functioning...' She gave a light laugh. 'That's sort of true. He forgets sometimes that not everyone has his energy levels.'

Lizzie digested this information in silence, gripped by unfamiliar and uncomfortable emotions. Whatever else her future husband was, he inexplicably appeared to inspire fierce loyalty from his employees.

Inexplicably, mocked the voice in her head. You mean other than his being sensitive and thoughtful?

Any problem could be worked through if you broke it down into manageable pieces. It was a philosophy that Adonis applied in practical terms every day of his life.

It was the same attitude he had approached his prospective marriage with, and so far everything had gone according to plan. He rejected the voice in his head that suggested this was only because he had avoided Lizzie Rose during the interim.

With her sharp tongue and her wicked sarcasm, not to mention that mouth, she was a disruptive influence to his peace of mind. He had never experienced a person who… He felt her presence like an internal pressure.

Obviously he could negate this, but it seemed reasonable to delay any time-consuming conflict until after the contract was signed.

Pushing the problem ahead does not make it go away, scorned that voice in his head.

The scornful voice was proved correct when he saw her walking towards him.

She hadn't opened her mouth yet and he was chained to the spot by nothing more complicated than lust as he felt a scalding streak of heat slide like a blade through his body and settle in his groin.

He had suspected what his bride had spent a lifetime hiding, but the reality was more in every sense of the word than he had imagined. And all of that more was showcased by the outfit she was wearing, a skirt and cropped jacket ensemble in pale blue.

The skirt that managed to swish and cling to her bottom ended three inches above her knee and showcased really incredible legs, which he instantly decided would be criminal to hide. The jacket was fitted with a tiny peplum that showed off a tiny waist and the feminine flare of her hips. Beneath, the cream corset affair was held together with a row of tiny pearl buttons; it had a square neckline that didn't distort the full curve of her dramatically incredible breasts.

He recognised the moment she identified him—her spine went significantly stiffer and her chin rose before she paused for a moment, putting down a basket she was carrying. She balanced on one leg while she removed a crepe-soled trainer and slid on a slingback spiky heel she had produced magician-like, then the balancing-on-one-foot routine was repeated.

The ground under her feet was even but Lizzie felt as if she were on a tightrope as she walked towards the tall waiting figure. Elegant to the nth degree in his dark formal suit and snowy white shirt, he looked as though he had just stepped out from the pages of a fashion shoot intended to make the gullible male believe if they too used this brand of hair product they would become utterly irresistible, have a beautiful woman in their bed and drive a designer car.

She blamed it on the heels, except of course no glossy fashion shoot had ever projected the sort of earthy sexual aura that Adonis did.

'Hello, nice day for it.' It wasn't but, as the other option had been help or, even worse, wow, Lizzie settled for gentle sarcasm.

He did look wow!

Actually, wow was an understatement. Lean and muscular, his carved features could have graced a statue, but they were real, glowing, alive.

She held herself tense as dark, heavy-lidded eyes that seemed to hold no expression flickered over her.

'You are not wearing the wedding dress.'

'Very observant of you. It's lucky I'm not, really, as I would have looked every kind of lunatic wafting through the arrivals lounge in white lace and frills.'

'I didn't think of that and there should not have been frills. I specifically mentioned that.'

His ready admission took the wind out of her lofty superior sails. She fell back on attack, it being the best form of defence, she really hoped, against the hormonal overload that was nibbling away at her ability to string words together that made sense. 'Well, neither did I, think, that is, because I didn't know I was about to get on a plane, because you didn't have the courtesy to inform me of your plans.'

'You told me to do what I liked. You were not interested,' he pointed out.

'Well, I didn't mean this…' She faltered, annoyed with him for paraphrasing her own parting shot against her. 'And Jenna went to the trouble of putting together an information pack for me and you didn't even bother to pass it on!'

'Did she?' he said, pretending ignorance. 'It must have slipped my mind.'

He had actually been on the point of pressing the send key on that information pack when he had hesitated, Jenna's comment when he had requested the schedule springing to mind.

'Most brides would prefer flowers.'

There was a balance between formal and flowery, and maybe the timetable was not hitting it, but then flowers would have been overkill too and possibly thrown back in his face. Decision-making was not something that Adonis struggled with, he didn't like the paralysing indecision, and in the end had opted for doing nothing.

He should have known that lack of action would not save him from her sharp tongue.

Lizzie snorted. 'You mean you wanted me to feel even more helpless and out of my depth than I already do!' She immediately regretted the fact she had just admitted a vulnerability to him that she had managed to deny even to herself.

'I don't want you to feel that way.'

'I don't,' she countered.

'You look stunning.'

Her defensive stance melted, as did her insides. Blue eyes met dark and the world seemed to still for the space of several heartbeats, until she brought her lashes down in a protective shield and mumbled, 'You look OK too.'

His brows lifted. 'Thank you, yes, we make a handsome couple, I think,' he concluded, making her think of some sort of preening, self-satisfied jungle cat sheathing his claws before he swiped her verbally with one satiny sharp paw.

'Jenna said there is an option of pausing to redo my lips, but it won't be necessary.'

Her comment brought his eyes to her mouth just as she moistened her lips nervously with the tip of her tongue. The flickering action, unintentionally erotic, sent a surge of reckless lust through his body.

Dmitri repeated his question three times before Adonis, thinking about how she would taste, reacted with a vague, 'Ah yes, fine, you go ahead, we'll follow.'

CHAPTER SIX

As HE TURNED back to Lizzie he focused his attention on the basket at her feet. 'What is that?'

He looked so bemused that the tension that had been building inside her vanished. This was a conversation she didn't mind having because there was only one outcome. The knowledge made her feel in charge.

'My cat.'

His thick dark brows knitted into a pattern of disapproval. 'You have brought a cat to a wedding.'

'Well, I couldn't leave her on the plane.'

She spoke kindly, as though she were addressing someone slightly slow on the uptake.

'Why was she on the plane in the first place?'

'Because we come as a package deal.'

Her tone, in fact her entire body language, suggested she wanted to instigate a fight, just for the hell of it, meek mouse… He felt quite wistful for the time when she was neatly filed under that heading in his head.

'Do you know how absurd you sound?'

'Do you actually think I care about what you think about how I sound or, for that matter, look?' She frowned, not liking the look of comprehension that spread across his face.

'This is about my remark at that awful dinner, isn't it?'

She opened her mouth to deny this and closed it again. 'You were extremely rude, but that came as no surprise.'

'You were wearing a tent-like garment, which for a woman with your shape is—'

'What's wrong with my shape?' she flared.

'Nothing in the world except the fact you try and hide it.'

Her pugnacious stance disintegrated in the space of a single thud of her heart, and her insides melted as she stared at the compelling earthy perfection of his carved patrician features.

'You should not try to hide your femininity. You should celebrate it.'

This advice, coming from a man who had never been seen in public with a woman who didn't have hip bones you could hang a coat hanger on—in fact, she decided viciously, women who were coat hangers—struck her as the ultimate hypocrisy.

'We were talking about my cat, not my body,' she reminded him coldly.

They might not be talking about her body, but he was thinking about it. The thoughts combined with the subtle citrusy scent of her perfume, and the surge of desire and something more complicated that he fought hard against all but consumed him.

'You were talking, correction, you were itching to start a pitched battle. You brought your damned cat. Fine. I have no view on it at all.' His dark eyes flickered to the basket she was brandishing like some bloody weapon. 'How about you and your pet get in the car and let's get married?' snarled the groom.

She fixed him with a killer glare.

'How can I resist such a charming invitation?'

She sat in the air-conditioned luxury barely registering it, or the scenery through the window, but there was only so long a person could sit stiff-backed without being in pain.

'I'm a bit nervous about this. I never thought I'd get married, let alone to someone who…to someone like you,' she said, her eyes trained on her interlaced fingers as her bottled-up feelings burst out. 'I keep telling myself it's not

real, but it bothers me so much that I am…
It's cheating.'

She leaned back into her seat, her temper
burned off, and a sadness remained.

He flicked her a sideways glance, noting the
traces of blue shadows under her beautiful eyes,
the quiver of the blue-veined pulse in her temple. He redirected his eyes to the road ahead, his
brain shifting gear to cope with the surge of protectiveness her vulnerability shook loose in him.

'Who are we hurting, Lizzie Rose?'

She blinked, her eyes swivelling to his achingly perfect profile. 'It's… I…' She paused,
struggling to put her complex feelings into
words. She couldn't bring herself to say that
marriage was a sacred thing because that
would have made her sound naive.

'You can walk away at any moment.'

Nostrils flared, she sucked up a quivering
breath and pushed out a resentful, 'Yes, I know
you're right.'

He laughed. 'That must have hurt.'

'Yes, actually it did, but the last week has
been…not easy.'

'Tell me about it.'

Her brow pleated into an uncomprehending
frown until understanding dawned and the
feeling in his voice made sense.

Just because he was pushing this didn't mean he liked it. How could he? He was facing a fake marriage of inconvenience with Deb's dumpy little cousin while he was still grieving for his lost love. It had to be dredging up all sorts of painful memories of the wedding day he had been robbed of.

'Sorry, it must be hard for you.' Did he feel disloyal to his lost love?

'Sorry?' He slid a mystified glance her way before focusing on the road ahead.

'I know… Well, I don't know.' How could she? She had never been in love. 'Deb was so beautiful, and your wedding would have been… This one isn't real.'

And when it was for real another man would unlock the fiery passion he sensed inside her, a fiery passion that he was sure that her lovers to this point had not tapped into.

Of course, with it came the stubborn streak, the awful dress sense and her misplaced empathy.

'The traffic is though.'

She clamped her lips. 'OK, sorry.'

'You've already said that. Sorry for what, exactly? You feel cheated from the big wedding you have always imagined?'

'God, no!' she came back with a horrified

shudder. 'I have never dreamt of a wedding at all, ever, but you…' A frustrated sigh left her lips. His attitude was making it very hard to hang onto her sympathy.

'You had Deb. It must be hard after you planned your perfect wedding. The contrast with—'

'Marriage is a contract.'

'Well, ours is, obviously, and I know it might not seem like it now, but one day you might— you will—meet someone.' And Lizzie for one did not envy the woman he would marry for real, not when competing with a ghost who would never gain a few inches around her waist or have a bad hair day.

'If you want to set me up with another woman while we are married, you might raise a few eyebrows.'

'I'm not trying to set you up. I'm being sympathetic,' she pushed out in an offended rush. 'I won't bother.'

'That news makes me very happy and, for the record, if I want a woman, I have never needed a cheerleader.'

'That is… You are…'

'Being very restrained. You notice I did not say pimp for me. So are you still up for this or shall I just, as they say, call the whole thing off?'

The question hung in the conditioned air between them for a long moment. She hardly trusted her voice as she sent him a poisonous sideways glare. 'No, let's do it.'

Adonis's firm lips turned up at the corners. He had known many women over the years who had been willing to go to any lengths to extract a proposal from him and he was marrying a woman who approached marriage to him with the enthusiasm most people reserved for a root canal or leaping into a lake of freezing water.

'In that case, have a look in the glove box. There's a ring. Put it on.'

'I don't need a ring.'

'It's not about need.'

Lizzie stared at the ring, nestled in red velvet, the sapphire surrounded by twinkling diamonds. A very expensive piece of window dressing, like the wardrobe of clothes.

'People will think I'm a cheapskate if you don't have an engagement ring.'

She flashed him a sideways look and warned, 'It won't fit.'

But it did.

Obviously it didn't, but it felt to Lizzie as though the long corridor went on for ever. The sound of her heels on the marble floor had a dreamlike quality as she fell into step beside Jenna, who looked almost as nervous as Lizzie felt.

Adonis was walking a little ahead, his head tilted as he made conversation with the person who appeared to be the celebrant. In truth, Lizzie had no idea because she had only heard one word in three when the woman had introduced herself above the static buzz that had taken up residence in Lizzie's head along with Adonis's distinctive deep voice and jumbled snatches of conversation.

One rose to the surface above the others.

He'd said she looked stunning.

She purposely dampened the illicit little glow of pleasure that came with the memory, reminding herself that he was not talking about her, he was talking about her clothes. She was still the same person she had been two years ago, he had just admired the fancy wrapping.

Which was of course shallow, but she had to admit that actually the feel of expensive silk and natural fibres against her skin was sensual... Normally, she was a sports bra fan, but the underwired piece of silk she was wearing was pretty and gently supportive.

She was still thinking about underwear and how he'd known her size when the corridor ended, and they reached a large arched metal-banded door.

There were no more thoughts to distract her from the moment. Her brain had effectively gone into frozen freeze-frame.

The celebrant stood to one side and Lizzie felt everyone's expectant eyes on her. The space next to Adonis was hers for the taking.

How many tall skinny women out there would envy her and feel quite rightly that they would be a better fit for that spot, for the ring on her finger? Her flickering gaze was captured by the ring as she began to tug panicky at it.

'What are you doing?'

'You can use this as a wedding band.'

'I have wedding bands for us both.'

'Oh, right...' It seemed he had thought of everything except the fact that no one would believe that he had picked her out for his bride.

The elephant in the room had never been properly addressed. The argument that should have been front and centre. Nobody was going to believe they were a fit. Everyone would see through the ruse. This would all be a stupid waste of time.

'Do you need a glass of water?'

That was Jenna and then another voice said something about nervous brides.

'I'm fine.' Her voice sounded as though it were coming from a long way away and her feet felt heavy as she finally walked towards him. Her stomach was a mess of butterflies as she kept her gaze low under the mesh of her naturally dark eyelashes.

She fell in beside him, close, but not quite touching as they walked through the arch into a flower-filled paved quadrangle enclosed by richly glowing stone walls, beyond which you got iconic glimpses of the Rock against a cerulean-blue sky, the Rock that dominated Gibraltar, that pretty much was Gibraltar.

Her heels on the stone sounded loud but the water falling from the fountain was louder.

'You've got no flowers,' Jenna suddenly exclaimed, sounding horrified.

As if flowers were the only absence in this wedding, Lizzie thought, turning a bitter laugh into a cough.

'There are plenty of flowers here,' she soothed, amazed that she sounded calm, almost normal. But it was true: a riot of colour spilled out of the raised beds, herbs flourished in the cracks between the stone slabs, filling the air with their aroma as they were crushed underfoot.

'She has a cat.'

Lizzie had hardly forgotten he was there but the sound of his deep voice made her jump.

'Give him to Dmitri.'

For once it didn't sound like an order. If he'd pushed it she would have hung on, but he didn't so she handed Mouse over, telling her to be a good girl.

'It's her, not him.'

'Would your cat like to run around? There is a secure area, the smaller garden, more intimate, some couples prefer that… If you like she could be released there to stretch her little legs. Suitable for animals. A couple last month had their rescue dog deliver the ring.'

'Oh, how lovely! So romantic!' Lizzie exclaimed, enchanted and at the same time depressed because of the contrast to her own wedding, but she still hesitated. 'It's secure? She couldn't escape?'

'Oh, absolutely not. Shall I?'

She nodded her permission to Dmitri, then smiled at the older woman. 'Thank you so much.'

While desperately aware of him at a cellular level, Lizzie didn't look at Adonis through the entire mercifully short ceremony—maybe because she was so aware.

If it hadn't been for the rapid rise and fall of her incredible breasts, he might have thought she had stopped breathing. She radiated stillness as she delivered her responses in a soft, barely audible voice, and not until the final moment did she abandon her still-statue pose and he saw a myriad emotions move across the surface of the vivid little face lifted to him.

She appeared almost to be compensating for his lack of emotional reaction. His teeth ground in frustration. It was almost as if she was trying to guilt-trip him.

To be cast in the role of villain to her victim did not sit well with him. She had not walked into this with her eyes closed, she knew what she was doing, he thought, feeding his anger to drown out the noise from his irrational guilty conscience. Totally irrational!

But she looked so lost.

He pushed the thought away. Just because a woman had big blue eyes and narrow, fragile wrists did not make her weak. He was not attracted by weakness in a woman, and Lizzie Rose was anything but weak. She had tenacity and a temper, which were two of the reasons he liked her.

He liked her.

He buried the acknowledgement that felt like

a weakness and told himself that she would be better off moving forward, thinking about the next stage of their plan and the big reveal with his family instead of broadcasting every little thing she was feeling. Everything.

Theos! It appalled him that someone wore their emotions so close to the surface. How did she survive like that, wearing her vulnerabilities like a neon sign, like an open invitation to take advantage?

Like you did?

'You may kiss the bride.'

He angled his head, bending down as his big hands landed on her shoulders, his intention clear.

She didn't panic, a fact she was proud of. Instead she brought her hands palm outwards at chest height and whispered quickly, 'You really don't have to.'

'It's kind of obligatory to kiss the bride,' he retorted drily, smothering a fresh flare of annoyance that he was the one putting the effort in. She had as much invested in this working as he had. 'It's just a kiss. Just close your eyes and pretend I'm the man of your dreams.'

She heard the undercurrent of irritation in his soft-voiced aside and was not fooled by the loving hand that tenderly stroked the loose strands of hair from her face and curled around her cheek. He was right, of course. She was making it a big thing when it really wasn't.

You carry on telling yourself that, Lizzie.

'I think there's standing room only in that particular club and I'm not good with crowds.'

'Ouch!' he huffed under his breath, relieved to see the antagonistic spark in her eyes as he moved in closer, the action effectively capturing her hands between their bodies.

At the first brush of his lips her wide blue eyes closed and she swayed towards him as though responding to some sort of magnetic tug.

The soft brush of his lips over hers could have stopped there had her lips not parted slightly... Did she kiss him back?

It was hard to know who was responsible for the clash of lips, teeth, and tongue in the hot breathless moments before his hands fell from her shoulders.

It was a mistake, obviously. There was no argument. But she tasted like strawberries, and her lush lips were silky and soft. He hadn't been able to resist exploring them...and the moist inner aspects of her mouth. He had wanted to explore every inch. The jolt back to reality was like an ice shower, physically painful.

They simultaneously stepped back. Her knees were shaking, and she looked at the two rings that now lay on her finger.

'I wasn't expecting…' Her glance lifted, her eyes zeroing in on his mouth. 'It's beautiful, the courtyard,' she tacked on, saving herself from further embarrassment.

He virtually had to prise her mouth away.

Her body burned with the shame of it, though actually if it had just been shame that she burned with, ached with, it would have been a lot simpler.

'I wasn't expecting it to be outdoors,' she elaborated. 'So pretty,' she trilled, senselessly.

The next part was a bit of a blur, laughter, the chinking of glasses—at least she retained the residual sense of self-preservation and settled for orange juice.

It was actually a relief to get back in the private jet. Mouse had obviously exhausted herself in her brief moments of freedom, so she curled on Lizzie's lap and went to sleep. Nobody had ever said she was not a survivor.

Lizzie envied her.

For God's sake, Lizzie, less of the drama-queen stuff. It's not like you're flying towards your doom, she told herself sternly as she

shifted restlessly in the comfort of her deep
leather seat, causing the cat to flex her claws
in protest against Lizzie's thigh.

'Sorry,' Lizzie soothed after an ouch as she
stroked the soft, silky fur, turning her gaze
to the window and the stream of clouds wafting by.

Fatigue held at bay by nerves washed over
her in waves, receding and advancing until the
long surreal day caught up on her and her eye-
lids closed.

Adonis walked into the cabin, intending to up-
date Lizzie on what to expect when they landed
in Xania, but she was asleep, the darned cat
curled up on her knee.

Considering he had decided the cat had been
brought along for the ride just to irritate him,
he felt rather good he had not risen to the prov-
ocation; it opened one eye and regarded him
with disdain before closing it again, the purring audible from where he stood.

He studied Lizzie Rose's sleeping face,
slightly flushed in repose. The lashes on her
wide-set eyes cast a shadow over the smooth
curve of her high cheeks. Her relaxed mouth
was stretched in a soft half-smile, a few strands
of glossy hair lay across her cheek, and the

jewel-encrusted slide that had pulled her hair away from her face on one side had slid down to the end of one silky strand.

He could only suppose that his lengthy celibacy was responsible for the ribbons of heat that threaded through his body as he looked at her, thinking of the warmth of her lips.

Initially the celibacy had been a natural reaction to Deb's sudden death and then later, when there was widespread speculation about the woman who would be her replacement and apparently heal his broken heart, he had felt a disinclination to fuel the media and gift publicity to the first woman to make it to his bed.

Or then again, maybe he had been too lazy to make the effort. Sex had become too easy, almost mechanical, boring.

There was nothing lazy about the kick of his libido as his eyes followed the long, graceful curve of her neck where the skin looked smooth as warm silk, and then lower, where one of the tiny pearl buttons had slipped free of the loop of fabric, exposing a modest but fascinating glimpse of her bra and an even more fascinating section of cleavage.

It could not be considered a bad thing to lust after your own wife, but it could, given their unique circumstances, be considered a complication. His fingers flexed as he pushed them into his pockets, the compulsion to touch so strong it was almost overwhelming.

Lizzie Rose's passion was buried beneath prickles and contradictions.

She opened her eyes. He saw the confusion in the deep blue depths and heard her wince as the cat, annoyed at having its sleep disturbed, dug its claws into her thigh.

'Ouch, Mouse...' She pushed her hand through her hair and herself up in her seat.

Adonis caught the jewelled hair clip before it hit the ground and handed it back to her.

'Thank you,' she said as he dropped it into her open palm. 'I must have fallen asleep.' She sat upright from her slumped position, smoothing the cat's fur as she did so, the action making her aware that her skirt had ridden up, showing far too much leg.

Surreptitiously pulling it down, Lizzie angled a small cautious smile up at him, noting that he was no longer wearing a jacket and the tie was gone, leaving a small vee of butterscotch-coloured skin exposed at the base of his throat.

She looked around the cabin and realised they were alone. 'Where are Jenna and Dmitri?'

'They stepped out for a moment. There were

only two parachutes, but they said they'd meet us there,' he explained, deadpan.

'Very funny.' She sniffed, arching an interrogative brow.

'They have gone through to the bedroom, to take a Zoom call.'

She wrinkled her nose at the explanation. 'That sounds very high powered.'

'No, personal. Their son, Robert, he needs routine. When he is in residential care, seeing them at the same times every day helps.'

She nodded at the explanation. 'I suppose having a disabled child can put a lot of strain on a marriage,' she mused.

Adonis took a leather seat opposite her as one of the attendants approached with a tray bearing coffee and sandwiches.

'Thought you might be hungry,' he said, before adding, 'I am.'

As the attendant left he leaned back and crossed one ankle over the other, letting his long legs stretch out. Despite his claim to be hungry he seemed in no hurry to address the food.

'Jenna's first marriage broke down because the father couldn't cope. Dmitri loves the kid. He is a great dad.'

Lizzie took a sandwich and waited until she

had swallowed a bite before speaking. 'Will your parents be there on the island?' What were they going to make of his unlikely choice of bride?

'My parents? That is extremely unlikely.'

Something in his tone made her ask. 'You don't get on?'

'Get on?' he mused, looking at her over the rim of a coffee cup. 'We get on fine now that I am no longer an inconvenience.'

She shook her head. 'I don't understand.'

'My parents always found that having a child in the picture got in the way of their great epic love story.' He heard himself explain and immediately wondered why he was revealing this private part of his history.

Some of the tension bunched in his shoulders fell away when a logical explanation for his soul-baring almost immediately revealed itself: they were about to play a couple who had just eloped—it made sense that she would know something about his history.

He turned a deaf ear to the annoying voice in his head that inconveniently pointed out that the only thing Deb had known about his parents was that, according to her, they both looked far too young to have a grown-up son.

'Your father resented the attention your

mother gave you?' Lizzie tried to keep her disapproval out of her voice. Not easy—the idea of
a jealous manchild filled her with angry contempt.

Adonis laughed, and the discordant sound
made her nerves jangle.

'If my mother has maternal instincts they
are well hidden. My parents both thought that
having a child was the worst thing they ever
did, though, I have to hand it to them, they did
not allow my existence to ruin their lives,' he
explained with a cynical shrug. 'They packed
me off to school when I was seven and I spent
most holidays on Xania.'

Horrified, Lizzie didn't know how to respond. After a moment she pushed out a
troubled, 'Hands-off parenting is a thing, I
suppose,' struggling to think of anything non-
judgemental to say to even partially excuse his
parents. 'But I'm sure they didn't really feel
like that.' Even if that were true, it was truly
terrible in her eyes that they had made their
child think they did, made him feel he was
unwanted.

An image of a young Adonis, dark eyes and
a mop of jet hair, slid into her head and her
anger heated once more.

'I am not reading between the lines. They

told me on more than one occasion that they wished I had never been born.'

He watched her eyes fly cartoon wide before narrowing into furious slits. Nostrils flared, she put the rest of her sandwich in her mouth and swallowed without chewing.

'How? Well, they are…?'

'In love,' he drawled with a sardonic grimace of distaste. 'A narcissistic match made in hell. They are totally obsessed with one another to the exclusion of the rest of the world. Their fights are things of legend and their making up—' He caught her horrified expression and clamped his mouth over further unnecessary reveals. 'Don't look so devastated,' he added, thinking there was a big difference in discussing some family details so she could act the role he had brought her here to play and serving up a sob story with a side-order invitation to wander around in his head.

'I actually liked school. It taught me to be independent.'

'I've heard people say that.'

'And you don't believe it.'

She shrugged. 'I hated school,' she revealed abruptly. 'Well, secondary school at least.' Maybe if she had not just lost her mum, her dad hadn't gone on his cruise because looking at her reminded him of his dead wife, and the only female influence in her life hadn't been the well-meaning housekeeper whose ideas of suitable clothes and guidance for a pre-teen-age girl had been firmly rooted in the fifties, it might have gone better.

She had not complained to him, but maybe her dad had sensed she was unhappy when he had persuaded Deb's mum to allow Deb to transfer to the same school, reasoning that her presence would help Lizzie. It hadn't worked out that way. Deb had arrived and instantly been the popular girl that everyone wanted to be with. Lizzie hadn't minded her cousin ignoring her. In fact it had been preferable to the occasions when she'd led the bullying.

'Why?'

'The usual,' she said, avoiding his eyes and shrugging. She was already regretting opening up this far.

'You are not a very trusting person, are you, Lizzie Rose?' he observed, studying her with an intensity that made her shift uneasily in her seat.

'I don't have much reason to trust you, do I? I don't really know you!'

The utter absurdity of saying this to the man you had just married struck her forcibly. She paused, biting her full lower lip between her teeth as she gathered her calm around her, pulling it tight like a comfort blanket. Now was not the time for thinking about what she had done. That time had gone. She just had to deal with the reality of the present.

'My mum died just before I started secondary school. I missed her.'

He watched her expression close down and realised the world of hurt behind the composed words.

'That must have been tough.'

Her jaw clenched as she thought, *Do not be nice to me*. Nasty she could take, but nice cut through the protective layers that she had built up over the years.

'I was not…cool. The school didn't have a uniform and, well, my clothes sense then was pretty much the same as it is now. I was a swot, and, well, you get the picture. But you learn coping techniques…' Her voice trailed away as she articulated this for the first time.

'Such as?'

'Never let the bastards see you cry.' She flashed him a defiant look. 'Oh, and, of course, when you're the butt of the joke play dim and laugh with everyone else. It comes in handy even now,' she mused drily.

The wave of protectiveness that rose up in Adonis was shocking in its intensity. 'Bastards,' he murmured. 'Or should that be bitches? Was your school mixed?'

'Mixed, and I went from flat-chested to… not flat-chested overnight.' Avoiding his eyes, she got to her feet and made a show of looking around for the cat. 'Where has she got to?'

On cue, Mouse revealed herself by leaping onto a startled Adonis's knee.

'Theos!'

His bass rumble of alarm made her laugh. He was looking at the cat with the sort of expression normally reserved for an unexploded bomb.

She silently thanked her scene-stealing moggy for affording a distraction.

'Let me take her.' She bent, loose strands of her hair brushing his cheek as she gathered the purring cat up in her arms. 'How long before we land?' she asked, looking around for the cat basket.

'Probably time to put it—' he caught her eye and corrected himself with a half-smile '—her in her basket.'

She nodded.

'You're nervous?'

Lizzie laughed, secured the cat in her basket

and turned, staring at the rings on her finger and feeling a contracting wave of fear swell in her chest. 'Of course I'm nervous. People will never believe that—'

'They will,' he contradicted, rising in one fluid motion to his feet. Towering over her, he placed his hands on her shoulders. 'They will believe because they will all want to believe. They will look at you and think you are exactly what I need.'

'What, someone plain and homely? I don't even know who they are other than your grandfather.'

'Homely?' he echoed before he threw back his head and laughed. He was still laughing when his hands dropped from her shoulders and he fell back into his seat in an elegant sprawl, all long legs, coordinated grace and off-the-scale sex appeal.

Lizzie planted her hands on her hips and glared down at him, using her anger to hold back the panic that was tight in the pit of her stomach. 'I'm glad you think this is funny.'

CHAPTER SEVEN

'NOT FUNNY. Tragic if you really believe that.' Adonis had stopped laughing and looked inexplicably annoyed. 'What have the men in your life been doing if you don't know that you are gorgeous?'

'I don't need men to tell me—' Lizzie stopped, colour flooding her face.

Gorgeous?

He made a sweeping motion with his hands, his dark eyes lingering on the sensual curves of her lush body. 'You are sexy, you have tremendous legs that you never allow anyone to see, you envelop your figure in tents and dull colours, but your body issues aside—' He pushed away the subject as though it had been nothing more controversial than the weather forecast.

'Aside from my grandfather, my two aunts will be there and their husbands, or in Elena's case not her husband yet, her divorce has not come through. Elena and Lydia are my father's twin half-sisters, considerably younger than him. They both have daughters, a set of twins apiece, teens.'

Lizzie blinked, taking the details on board. 'So what did they say when you told them we were coming, that we are…' she cleared her throat, finishing on a shrill '…married?'

'Nothing.'

She looked at him blankly.

'I didn't tell them and I hadn't confirmed I would make it for the birthday party.'

'Birthday party?' she said, trying to stay calm.

'My grandfather is eighty today.'

She stared at him, then gave an incredulous bubble of laughter and sank back into her seat.

'So you are just going to walk in and announce…?' She gasped, shaking her head in disbelief. 'You really do like making an entrance, don't you?' Not for one second did she think the timing was accidental. 'For the record, I don't.' But then she reflected, shaking with the strength of her feelings, Adonis was not interested in what she liked, wanted, or needed.

Before he could respond, Jenna and Dmitri reappeared.

Adonis turned his head. 'How was Robert?'

Jenna nodded and smiled. 'He's settled in really well. Right,' she added with a grimace. 'Time to belt up?' She sighed and closed her eyes. 'Wake me when it's over.'

'Adonis.'

He turned back to his bride and found azure-blue eyes fixed unblinkingly on his face. 'Lizzie.'

Her lips tightened. 'Let me get this right—we are going to crash a birthday party and tell your nearest and dearest we are married.'

'That's about right, though first you can get changed. I picked out a couple of possibles and laid them out on the bed.'

'I'm not letting you pick out my clothes!' What her voice lacked in volume, it made up for in outrage.

He responded with a teeth-grating gorgeous smile that made her want to hit him.

'Why would you do this?' she despaired. 'Why land me on them this way? Couldn't you come up with something less…dramatic?'

'You forget that our engagement has already been announced, even if not by us, so it's hardly going to be a drama. There might be some ruffled feathers that we robbed them of a wedding, but eloping has the cachet of being romantic,' he drawled with a lip curl that suggested he did not share this viewpoint. 'The old man had the element of surprise. He'd taken control of the narrative but now it is our turn.'

'Don't include me in this,' she said, leaning forward in her seat to fix him with a killer glare. 'It has nothing to do with me.'

'The ring on your finger says otherwise,' he countered. 'Look, what is the issue? Keeping this a secret rather defeats the object of the exercise.'

'Obviously I didn't want to keep it a secret.'

He arched a sceptical brow. 'So what is the problem?'

'You playing some sort of game with your grandfather, proving you are in charge, watching people dance to your tune. You are as manipulative as he is.'

Her chest heaving as she struggled to contain her feelings, she slid a cautious sideways glance at the other couple in the cabin and was relieved that they seemed oblivious to the war of attrition being waged across the aisle.

'Did it occur to you for one second to imagine how I am going to feel being thrown to the lions this way?' she hissed resentfully. 'A family party!'

'No one is going to eat you. You will be fine,' Adonis said, his infuriating attitude of lazy indifference tipping over into impatience as he advised her to, 'Just relax and fasten your seat belt.'

A glance through the window told her the tarmac was empty apart from another jet with the distinctive gold Aetos logo on its side. It would seem that there would be no massive queues to negotiate and the only officialdom for a man who literally had his name written on everything would involve bowing and scraping, she concluded cynically.

'Aren't you coming with us?' Lizzie asked, hiding her panic under a smile when Dmitri and Jenna made their farewells.

She struggled to hide her escalating dismay when they explained they would be going straight to the bungalow they were staying in for the duration.

'We're officially on holiday now,' Jenna said, adding a comforting, 'You'll be fine.'

Lizzie nodded and made her way to one of the bedrooms—apparently the jet boasted two—where there was a selection of the promised outfits laid out on the bed.

She stripped down to her bra and pants, feeling as creased as the suit she took off and hung on a hanger. After a short internal debate she ignored the shower in the en suite but felt slightly fresher after splashing her face with water and refreshing her make-up.

It didn't take long—a few minutes later she was viewing the results with a critical eye, the fresh gloss of lipstick, a smudge of shadow on her lids and, because she did look desperately pale, a light dust of blusher on the apples of her cheeks. She decided she looked less ghostlike, though the sprinkling of freckles across her nose and cheeks still shone through.

Bending her head forward, she shook out her long hair. The silky and tangled strands almost swept the floor as she bent down and began to brush in long, rhythmic strokes that made her glossy rich hair crackle with static. After one final brush, she straightened up, pushing the mane of hair back from her face with one forearm as she stepped into the bedroom.

The breath left her lungs in a sibilant hiss as Lizzie found herself looking at her new husband, who was in the act of fighting his way into a fresh white shirt. It hung open, revealing the carved musculature of his tanned chest complete with a light sprinkling of body hair and the muscle-ridged corrugation of his flat washboard belly. She licked her lips, unable to stop her eyes following the narrow directional arrow of dark hair that vanished beneath the belt of his dark tailored trousers.

In seconds the creeping heat in the pit of her stomach became a flaming inferno, the tug of her sex between her legs a throbbing ache and inside the silky cups she could feel her nipples shamelessly harden into tingling peaks.

Sensing that his dark hooded eyes had landed on this shameful physical response and painfully aware of the liquid heat in her pelvis—it felt as though she were being attacked on multiple fronts—she lifted her hands in a defensive gesture to cover her breasts, stopping midway when she realised it would make the situation a million times worse by drawing attention to her weakness.

Mortified, confused and angry that it was now of all the times for her libido to come out of hibernation, she drew in a ragged breath and lifted her gaze. Unfortunately the level of her thoughts did not follow.

'Sorry, I… Sorry,' she mumbled, not caring if she sounded stupid, just glad whole words came out.

Adonis didn't hear what she said. His mind was filled with the imagined sound of her gasp as his tongue slid between her lips. The muscles in his brown throat worked visibly as he held her gaze in a blank burning stare while inside his head he was seeing those soft curves plastered up against him. There was a whole series of incrementally more erotic fantasy images being projected by his imagination onto his retina.

He had thought of her as a revelation, but now he knew that barely came close to describing her body. How could any man look at her and not think of sinking into the softness, feeling her warmth close around him?

'I left my shirts in here,' he finally pushed out hoarsely, glancing at the crumpled discarded shirt on the bed then back at Lizzie, immediately seeing her on the bed, her arms outstretched to him.

Adonis could feel his control unravelling faster by the second. He knew he had to remove himself from this situation or... Before he could come up with the or option, there was a tap on the door.

As he pushed it open to reveal one of the male attendants standing there looking apologetic, Lizzie grabbed for her robe and moved out of view.

The conversation was short and inaudible to Lizzie, who had regained a crumb of her composure. When he stepped back inside, she coached the belt on the robe another painful hitch tighter.

'Take your time. No hurry, we are not on the clock.'

'Thanks, yes, of course...'

He vanished and she lowered herself to the floor in a cross-legged posture that spoke a lot for her core strength. Lizzie was not thinking about core strength, she was not thinking at all, she was stunned, shocked and... She had never felt anything approaching that before, not the wanting to touch, to taste... She wanted to surrender not just to the need inside her but to him.

She took a deep breath and told herself to get a grip as, with thoughtless elegance, she rose to her feet and focused on the practical.

She needed to get dressed.

She didn't take her time. She didn't even look at the dresses laid out on the bed. Heart hammering—what the hell had just happened there?—she grabbed the one nearest.

Like you don't know, mocked the voice in her head.

Maybe the colour caught her eye. It was a deep jewelled turquoise blue; the heavy silky fabric skimmed elegantly and didn't cling but managed to show every dip and curve of her body.

Still feeling dazed, she glanced in the mirror and a stranger looked back at her. She would have walked past this Lizzie in the street and not recognised herself, not that walking past yourself was an option unless you had a twin. With a supreme effort she closed down her tangled jumble of thoughts and looked properly. Ignoring the sultry glow in her eyes and the light all-over flush on her skin, she took in the simplicity of the dress that ended with a sensual swish four inches above her knee.

It was a simple tunic in cut but subtly shaped to show her narrow waist, the deep vee on the back showed her shoulder blades, and it was high in the front but still revealed the delicacy of her collarbones. The pleated cap sleeves that floated when she moved provided the drama.

She had never imagined she could look either elegant or sexy, but in this dress she looked both. The spiky heels with the pointy toes and the frivolous bow didn't diminish the effect. She really did have quite decent legs, she decided as she contorted to see her rear view in the mirror.

The effect could have given her confidence, and it did, to a point. It helped with the illusion she was acting a part. The problem was that she hadn't been acting just then. Her stomach flipped, and her body thrummed with the memory and intensity of those moments. She had felt attraction before but not the inexorable tug of animal magnetism, chemistry. Come on, Lizzie, she told herself impatiently. Sex.

She was inexperienced but she was not stupid or blind and he had felt it too, or something. Even as she remembered the feral heat in his eyes, the tension that surrounded him like an aura sent an illicit thrill of fluid heat through her body.

She exited the plane alone, apart from Mouse in her basket. Lizzie held onto her tight, as though she were her only link to reality, to who she really was. Adonis was already in the sleek car waiting for her. Thinking he might be watching made her determined not to trip, so she focused on putting one foot in front of the other.

So long as she thought about feet she would be OK.

'That cat travels well.'

Her eyes flickered to the basket wedged by her feet. 'She is resilient, one of life's survivors. Are there any other cats in the…?' She paused and realised she didn't have a clue where they were headed. The sun was dropping, the sky illuminated by streaks of gold, and every so often she had a glimpse of the sea tinged with gold.

'Villa,' he supplied, aware in the periphery of his vision as she crossed her legs; the silky rustle that went with the action aroused him to a painful degree.

'I really don't know. When you hand him over to the kitchen staff...'

Lizzie embraced her anger with a kind of relief. It was marvellous to be able to think he was shallow and lacking in any sort of empathy, not how gorgeous and incredible he smelled.

'I am not about to hand her over,' she snapped, outraged at the suggestion.

'You do know that you are being ridiculous.' The residual tension from the moments when she had been standing there in her very provocative underwear had lessened but not diminished. It had more coalesced into a tight fist of frustration and resentment in his gut.

Lizzie turned her head, intending to project cold ice queen, but an iceberg could not have cooled the angry frustrated heat inside her. If her eyes had been lasers his perfect profile would be seriously damaged. 'I'm not discussing this.'

'Fine, my suite... The sitting room opens out onto a quadrangle, totally enclosed. Will that suit you and your blasted animal?' he asked in a clipped tone.

Lizzie's lips tightened in response to the sarcasm in his voice. 'Yes.' She stopped. 'Your suite? Where will I be?'

'We are arriving a married couple. Where the hell do you think you will be?'

Her breath coming in shallow laboured puffs, she didn't say a word for a moment. 'I hadn't thought that far ahead.'

'Sometimes it is better not to. Thinking is not all it is hyped up to be. You can't always factor in the...' The fact that he wanted her, so badly that it felt like a weight in his chest. 'Look, we are married. We will be sharing a room. Let's work out the logistics later. It might not be an issue.'

She let the heavy silence lie for a moment. 'What do you mean?'

An exasperated hiss emerged through his clenched teeth. 'You know exactly what I mean. I am attracted to you and you feel the same way. It could make the next few weeks enjoyable or it could make them a lot less comfortable. Frustration makes you quite tetchy.'

'I'm not frustrated!' she exploded. 'I'm confused. Someone like you does not want someone like me.'

'For pity's sake, move on!' he bellowed.

She closed her eyes until he had negotiated a bend at what felt to her like reckless speed.

'I don't know what the guys you have been sleeping with have been doing.' His lips curled in disgust. 'But I promise you they have been doing it wrong if you don't know… *Theos!*' he grated. This woman was driving him to places he had never been before. His brief sideways glance was at the upper end of smoulder. 'How incredibly sexy you are.'

She sat there, the numb shock giving way to a sense of power she had never experienced before, a power that came from knowing that a gorgeous man wanted you.

Well, he had to. She could think of no reason for him to lie.

'And you'd do it right?' she heard herself throw out recklessly.

If the stare he aimed at the road ahead had been directed at her, Lizzie imagined she would have ignited.

'Damned right I would.'

His arrogance should have offended her. It didn't because she believed him with every fibre of her being.

The car jolted, sending up a shower of loose gravel as he brought it to a halt.

At her feet the cat squealed, but Lizzie didn't have time to soothe it. She opened her mouth but the sound was smothered by his lips, lost in the heat. The carnality of the way he claimed her mouth, licked into the moist warmth, flicked, teased and sucked. The sheer undreamt-of dizzying pleasure left her shaking.

Adonis looked into her glazed eyes, gave a fierce nod of satisfaction and restarted the engine.

She had to say something, and he had been upfront about the fact he was some sort of sex god.

'I'm a virgin.'

The car came to another screaming halt, followed by a stream of invective in several languages that you didn't need to be a linguist to translate as not polite.

'You're a…?'

She nodded, deciding she would remember Adonis looking shaken because she doubted it occurred often.

'How is that even possible?'

'It wasn't a criminal offence last time I checked,' she snapped back, not enjoying him acting as if she was a freak, even though there were occasions she felt she might be.

'I refuse to believe you have an issue with sex.'

Well, if she ever had, that ship had quite definitely sailed now, she thought, moistening her tingling lips. 'No, I have an issue with…well, the emotional bit…love…and I wasn't sure that I could have one without the other. I might,' she added, looking at his mouth, 'have been wrong.'

It was true he was the last man in the world she would have fallen in love with, but she could definitely have sex with him so long as she knew he wasn't thinking of Deb. That would for sure be a lust killer.

'Love?' he said as though he needed her to translate.

'I am not brave enough to love someone and then lose them for whatever reason. Why would anyone open themselves to that world of hurt?'

'I don't sleep with virgins. I have never slept with a virgin.'

She lowered her eyes, making a supreme effort to be adult about the rejection. 'A bit like skiing, I suppose. Nursery slopes are a bit boring for people used to going off-piste.'

He vented an incredulous laugh. 'You do know that you say the most… I think an hour in your head would make any man…' His voice trailed off as his mind made the leap from head to bed, razor blades of lust leaving a zigzag-ging trail of destruction in their wake. 'I think we should have this discussion later.'

When he was not fantasising about back-seat or, for that matter, front-seat sex. What was he, a teenager? A virgin. He had never spent much time thinking about virgins. There was an abundance of women who were not, and the responsibility was something he had always avoided. He had always prided himself on being more evolved than men who got a kick from the idea of being a woman's first lover.

It turned out his smugness had been mis-placed. He wasn't so evolved, after all. All it took was the perfect storm, and a particular virgin.

It seemed to Lizzie that there wasn't that much to discuss but she shrugged and made no objection when he restarted the car.

Conversation was sparse on the rest of the journey—actually it was non-existent—but as the Aetos residence came into view Lizzie gasped.

The building, a sprawling white affair, had a low profile. It seemed to be built into the hill-side, organically almost a part of it, but de-signed so that most every window in the place, and there were many, appeared to face the sea.

He had slowed, appearing to appreciate the impact that first glimpse offered.

As they got closer she took in the other details in the fading light: the softly terraced gardens that ran right down to the beach, the paddocks below the escarpment the house was built into with horses galloping, tails up, as they passed. The glimmer of a swimming pool behind a row of sentinel pines against the darkening night sky.

'You spent your childhood here?' She didn't wait for him to respond. 'It really is a paradise.'

As he pulled up onto a gravelled forecourt and walked around the car to open the door for her, Lizzie could hear the sound of music drifting on the soft, salty, pine-tinged breeze.

She stepped out carefully on her heels, murmuring comforting things to Mouse, who was sniffing the air.

Adonis, outlined against the darkening sky, looked heart-stoppingly gorgeous as he took her elbow in a light supportive grip.

'You OK to do this?'

He watched as the turquoise silk reacted to her deep breath, making the fabric quiver deliciously and causing his libido to strain against the shackles he had imposed. Then the little chin lift that for some crazy reason made things inside him soften as she responded to the challenge with a 'bring it on' smile that didn't reach her eyes, which remained shadowed with trepidation.

Not enjoying his perceptive appraisal, she shrugged her narrow shoulders. 'I'd prefer root-canal work, but, as we're here, let's get it over with.'

Theos, this woman had balls, he decided with reluctant admiration. She was the equal of any adversary he had ever come up against, and she was on his side…for now.

He liked the idea of it staying that way. From somewhere surfaced a feeling he had never experienced before: he wanted her to like him.

Someone appeared before they had reached the massive double oak doors, which swung open.

'The place is wired for sound,' he whispered, still holding her elbow as they stepped forward.

Lizzie had no idea if he was joking or not, but she couldn't have laughed at that moment if her life had depended on it.

'Luisa…' The rest was Greek to Lizzie, quite literally.

After a few moments back and forth Adonis appeared to remember her existence.

'This is my wife, Lizzie Rose. Lizzie, this is Luisa, who has known me since I was…?'

The woman held her hand a little above knee level.

'I was never that small.'

His grin was so natural, so uncomplicated and so warm, it made him seem unfamiliar. Lizzie felt her chest tighten with an unnamed emotion.

'You are welcome. It makes my heart light to see Adonis with you.' She stepped back and pressed a hand to her chest. 'Yes, I can feel your love.'

Emotional tears stood out in her eyes.

Lizzie didn't dare look at Adonis. She hoped he felt as uncomfortable and guilty as she did. It was one thing to trick his grandfather, but not this nice woman. It seemed too unkind.

This was not a good start from her point of view—for starters, she was a terrible liar.

'We are here for the party. Are we too late for the fun?'

Without picking up on the sarcasm Lizzie could hear in his voice, the woman rushed in to cheerily assure him. 'Never, never. I will organise... Oh, this will make your grandfather so happy.'

Well, his grandfather might be a monster, but he obviously had one fan at least. The woman's sincerity was unmistakable.

'How is he today?'

'The pain,' Luisa began with a grimace. 'It makes him short-tempered.'

'Shorthand for he has been giving everyone hell.' Adonis frowned, his voice hardening as he tacked on, 'Does he not have adequate pain relief?'

'That I cannot say, but the doctor has been with him most of the day. He is here tonight as a guest. I do know your grandfather does not take his medication always as he should. He says he needs to stay alert.'

Adonis dragged a frustrated hand through his dark hair and ground out something angry in his native tongue, a look of grim determination spreading across his lean face as he nodded in thoughtful response to this information.

'We will see about that. Oh, Luisa. Lizzie's cat.'

The woman, who Lizzie was assuming held the role of housekeeper, looked at the cat basket that Lizzie had placed on the floor for the duration of the interchange.

'Shall I take him?' she said, moving forward.

'No!' Lizzie said before softening her abrupt response with a smile and adding, 'I prefer to keep her with me.'

Adonis restrained the impatient response

on the tip of his tongue. He was learning that Lizzie was not someone who reacted to orders well. 'I think the small sitting room in my suite might suit her until she gets her bearings, and the courtyard. Would you say that is a safe space?'

'Oh, yes, definitely.'

'Fine, then. Our luggage is in the car.'

'That is already being attended to.'

'Actually, Mouse is not an escape artist—she doesn't wander,' Lizzie said in defence of her pet.

'In that case might she not be more comfortable being released while we eat dinner?'

She tipped her head in reluctant acknowledgement that he was probably right. 'All right.'

'Then we will detour on the way to dinner.'

'Shall I tell your grandfather you are here?'

'No, let's not spoil the surprise.'

'This way, Lizzie.'

From the square hallway with its cool marble floors and cedar-panelled high ceiling, Adonis led her through a network of wide corridors, many with windows that revealed glimpses of spotlit gardens and moonlit sky. The floors underfoot were a mosaic of tiles or wood, and art on the walls provided blasts of colour and texture that she could have spent hours perusing. It went by in a blur.

'This is the link corridor to my private apartments,' Adonis explained as they entered what appeared to be a glass-walled box. Beyond her own reflection Lizzie could see the sea, silver in the moonlight apart from a few fingers of red that remained from the sinking sun, which vanished as she watched.

'That was…is beautiful.'

'Yes,' he murmured.

When something in his voice made her lift her head she found he was looking at her, not the silvered sea. His eyes appeared dark shadows, but the fierce tension stamped in the planes of his handsome face sent her stomach into a deep dive.

'Come.'

The spell was broken so thoroughly she thought she had imagined it as she followed him through the glass box. The door on the other side led into what appeared to be a study with book-lined walls, a large table and a big leather chair positioned to face a wall of French doors. He walked through it and into an adjoining room.

'This is the sitting room. I thought it might be appropriate for your cat.'

It would have been appropriate for visiting

royalty, Lizzie reflected, looking curiously around the minimally but tastefully furnished generous space. Like the previous room, there were French doors and, beyond them, she could make out a space that made her think of their wedding.

Was it really only hours ago?

Her eyes alighted on the fluffy little cat basket she had packed and Mouse's food and water bowls.

'How did this get here already?' she asked, putting the cat basket down and giving a sigh of relief.

'A heavy comfort blanket,' he mused, watching her.

'She is—' she began and stopped. 'OK, maybe a bit,' she admitted, thinking that she might as well invite him into her head because he had a disturbing habit of appearing there uninvited. 'How did all this get here before us?' she asked, opening the cat door.

'Luisa runs an ultra-efficient ship. She's not coming out.'

'She is essentially lazy and very adaptable. Any place with food and me is home for her.'

'You are her home?'

'Well, you know what I mean.'

He shook his head. He didn't. The idea of a

person rather than a place being home was an alien concept to him.

'The bedroom is through there,' he said as he saw her staring curiously at the ajar door. 'Check it out.'

Lizzie didn't immediately react to the invitation.

'I never ravish women before dinner.'

She refused to blush. 'Well, that's so civilised of you. The press tell so many lies about you it's scandalous.'

He grinned, immediately looking impossibly attractive, and waved a hand in gracious invitation.

Struggling to fight off a smile, she accepted the invite, walking past him and into another high-ceilinged, massive room.

While she was determinedly not looking at the huge four-poster bed that dominated the room, she immediately saw more illustrations of the efficiency Adonis had spoken about.

Through the open doors of the walk-in wardrobes she could see her new clothes hanging, other items neatly stacked on shelves.

'This is the bedroom,' he said, rather unnecessarily.

She didn't turn. The feeling of him so close was making her deeply uneasy.

'There is a dressing room through that way. I do not encourage people to unpack for me.' He opened a door and she saw his luggage on the floor. 'And the bathrooms are off that corridor,' he added, pointing to the right. 'The guest bedroom and bathroom are behind that. I don't need much space.'

Lizzie hid a smile. The scale of the rooms was…well, generous hardly covered the cavernous proportions. What, she wondered, would he consider generous space?

Walking back into the sitting room, she wondered whether he had noticed the discreet litter tray that was an addition to the elegant room, but decided not to mention it. The cat was sitting on the back of a sofa, cleaning herself.

'Be good,' Lizzie said before she pasted on a smile and blew a kiss her way.

CHAPTER EIGHT

LIZZIE REALISED THEY were retracing their steps, then they weren't, and she was hopelessly lost. The place was a beautiful maze. There were few steps, but the floor beneath her feet occasionally sloped.

Adonis could feel the tension coming off her.

'Greeks are friendly people. They love strangers.'

'Pardon my scepticism, but you are the only example I have.'

He conceded the strike with a wry grin. 'We love them so much we have a word for it.'

'A word for what?' They had reached a set of open double doors, and the echo of music she had heard was now a solid sound. Lizzie could see a jazz quartet at the far end responsible for the mellow sounds.

'For our love of strangers. *Filoxenia.*' His eyes brushed her pale face, lingering on the pulse beating at the base of her throat. 'OK?'

As OK, she thought, as she was likely to be. 'He won't believe that we are—'

'What he believes is not relevant, the point is he can't disprove anything, unless we tell him.'

'You must really not like him.'

'I love him. I want him to live his last days and weeks with the hope that there will be a grandchild and the challenge of disproving it will give him endless pleasure.' A distraction from dying, Adonis thought, his expression sombre.

'That seems perverse,' she observed, shaking her head.

'Possibly,' he conceded with a lazy grin. 'But that is the sort of family we are. Are you ready to do this?'

She nodded, thinking, I hope that room is filled with a lot of *filoxenia*. 'This is what I signed up for.' Obviously she had not been in her right mind.

She was glad of the encouraging hand on the small of her back as she stepped forward. The room was dominated by a long table lit by a row of chandeliers that picked out the silver and crystal, illuminating the edges of petals in the flower arrangements that were starting to wilt.

Lizzie really identified with those petals!

She wanted to shrink into his side, but pride stopped her.

Adonis appeared to have no problem with being the focus of attention. He ignored the various levels of bleats and gasps of surprise as he walked down the table to the head where a thickset man sat. He had a head of dark hair liberally streaked with silver and a face that cynicism had etched deep lines into.

'Happy birthday, Papou.'

'You have brought me a present?'

Lizzie felt the dark eyes move over her in an assessing sweep that made her want to crawl out of her skin.

'I have.' Adonis made a flourishing gesture towards Lizzie, like a magician pulling a rabbit out of a hat. 'My wife. And my thanks for introducing me to her. Lizzie Rose. Lizzie—' the fingers on the small of her back spread, as did the comforting warmth she needed at that moment '—this is my grandfather, Spyros.'

The silence was total. Even the musicians, awake to the drama of the moment, had stopped playing.

'Happy birthday. I hope you don't mind us gatecrashing?'

The elderly patriarch got to his feet, the hand tight on the arm of his chair the only indication that it was not easy for him. Despite his obvious ill health, he was not a man it was easy to pity.

'Welcome to our family.' He tilted his head towards Lizzie and gave what she supposed was his version of a smile. 'Elizabeth.'

'Lizzie.' He took the correction with a shrug that made her think a little of Adonis. 'I think you might know my father?'

She looked such a picture of innocence as she threw out the challenge that Adonis had to fight back an admiring laugh.

His grandfather didn't miss a beat. 'Indeed, I do. Welcome, Lizzie. Welcome to our home and this family.' He gestured in a grand fashion to the family seated around the table, who obediently echoed him.

'Sit by us, Adonis, sit by us!'

Lizzie was surprised the plea came from the two youngest of the family members. She had never thought that Adonis would bother to make himself popular with youngsters.

His grandfather responded to the children in Greek. His imperative gesture making it obvious that if anyone was going to have Adonis's ear it was him.

The girls, after a quick glance at the woman

sitting opposite them, subsided into sulky silence.

'Let me make the introductions. Lizzie, this is my aunt Elena.' He pointed out the tall, elegant woman whose dark hair had a striking silver streak. She nodded, her expression curious but not unfriendly.

'Her girls, Cora and Chloe, and her husband, Nik.'

A balding middle-aged man got to his feet and tipped his head in Lizzie's direction. *'Kalispera.'*

'This is my aunt Lydia.' The other woman had the silver streak but her face was much more rounded. 'And her girls—or should I say young women?'

'Yes, you should.'

'Definitely you should.'

'Hi, Lizzie,' they both said in unison. Then the one who had shaved off the sides of her hair added, 'I love that dress!'

'And this is Iris and Areti.'

'I'm Alex,' the man sitting closest to her said, getting to his feet and extending his hand. 'Better known as Iris and Areti's dad.'

'My soon-to-be ex-husband,' Lydia added as her husband sat down. 'And this is my partner, Adrian.' The handsome young man sitting

next to her sent Lizzie a dazzling smile. 'Dr...
Baros, is it?'

A tall, thin man wearing spectacles got to
his feet and inclined his head politely to Lizzie.
'Yassas.' He turned to Adonis. 'Congratula-
tions.'

'And that is the lot, except, of course, for
Grandfather.'

The music began at the same time as groups
of servers began to unobtrusively lay extra
places at the table and the rest of the family
discovered their voices.

Lizzie exhaled, finding the low buzz of chat-
ter a relief.

Adonis ushered her to one of the new place
settings and pulled out the chair for her, bending low to speak encouragingly into her ear.
'All OK?'

The whisper of his warm breath on her skin
sent a distracting wave of heat along her nerve
endings as his dark eyes held hers for a moment. She was incapable in that moment of
doing anything else but nod—she would have
nodded to anything he suggested. This piece
of self-knowledge she could have done without
and did nothing to soothe her jangling nerves.

'When you have finished, Adonis.' His

grandfather gave a sharp nod to the place that had been set beside him.

Before Adonis had taken his seat, Spyros pushed out a peremptory question, making no attempt to lower his voice. 'Now tell me, is it true? Are you actually married or is this one of your—?'

'We are married.'

'Oh, when?' one of the older twins asked. 'We could have been bridesmaids.'

'Today.'

The look of astonishment was shared by everyone at the table.

'You got married today? Where? How?' His grandfather continued to look sceptical.

'Gibraltar.' Adonis produced a paper from his pocket that Lizzie hadn't known he was carrying. Clearly he had anticipated some scepticism. 'The official licence will follow in a couple of weeks.'

'You eloped?' Lydia gasped.

'That is so romantic,' one of her daughters inserted, her twin nodding in vigorous agreement.

'Exactly, and Adonis is not one of life's romantics,' her mother responded, looking across the table to her sister for confirmation.

'It's true, he isn't.'

'I am pleased that I have enabled you two to agree on something.'

His aunts glared at him.

'So the engagement announcement was real?'

The doctor scraped his chair on the floor. 'Perhaps I should leave the family—'

'Sit down, man!' his patient instructed. 'If you breathe a word of what is said in this room, I will sue your pants off.'

Flushing, the medic sat down.

'The engagement announcement was true?' Elena said slowly. 'None of us believed it.'

'Neither did we,' Adonis said, sending Lizzie an intimate smile that left her shaking and reflecting on what a loss he was to the acting profession.

'Look, I really don't know why this marriage is anyone's business but our own. When you, Papou, conspired to push Lizzie Rose and I together...'

All eyes went to the figure at the head of the table, who simply shrugged.

'It was both our intentions to tell you to go, very respectfully of course, to hell. However, being thrown together as we were...the unique circumstances. I had never met a woman like

Lizzie.' The last observation had the ring of truth because, he realised, it was the truth.

One of the teen twins gave a sigh. Lizzie struggled to put a name to the pretty face but the names were still interchangeable in her head. 'I think that is so romantic.'

Unlike the teen, Lizzie had heard the deliberate ambiguity in his sentence, but she also heard the caressing lie and, even knowing it was a lie, she felt herself reacting to the fake warmth even though they had no intimate bond and never would be likely to have.

'We are planning on spending the rest of the summer here—'

'I'm not planning on dying yet,' the old man snarled.

'That is good to hear,' Adonis said smoothly, glad to see the spark of defiance while planning to discuss that subject with the doctor, who was looking fixedly at his plate as though wishing himself elsewhere.

Not an encouraging sign.

He had actually been shocked to see the changes wrought by the cruel disease that had had his grandparent in its claws the past few weeks. The clothes that hung on his broad frame, the sallow cheeks and dark shadows under his sunken eyes.

'Papa,' began Lydia.

'Do not "Papa" me, woman. I can't be doing with weaselly words. We all know I am dying.' He rose unsteadily to his feet. 'I will go to bed.'

His daughters both jumped to their feet.

'No, you can walk with me,' he said, waving an imperious finger at Lizzie.

'Papou…' began Adonis, rising to his own feet, his height and physicality highlighting the older man's frailty.

'No, Adonis,' Lizzie said calmly as she pushed her chair back.

'You haven't eaten—'

'I'm really not hungry.'

His eyes held hers, a question and concern in the dark depths. 'Sure?'

She nodded, determined not to let anyone think that she needed protecting, although the fact that this had been his instinct sent a warmth through her.

'My grandson seems mightily protective about you,' the old man commented as he paused to catch his breath after a few yards.

'I think he's worried I'll say the wrong thing… I do that.'

The admission drew a rumble of laughter from the old man's chest, which was followed by a bout of wracking coughs.

Lizzie waited.

'You are not much like your cousin.'

'No, Deb was very beautiful.'

He scanned her face as though searching for something. Lizzie endured the fierce scrutiny in silence.

'So you don't have a lover in the wings?'

Lizzie was more confused than offended. Her brows went up. 'A lover? I don't—'

'I wouldn't want my grandson's heart to be broken.'

Lizzie shook her head. 'I won't break Adonis's heart. I can promise you that,' she said.

'And do you always tell the truth?'

'That depends.'

'So you don't think that honesty is always the best policy?'

'Not if the truth hurts someone and would not achieve anything.'

Though he didn't immediately respond, Lizzie had the feeling she had said the right thing.

'So would you lie to my grandson?'

'Adonis is not an easy man to lie to.'

Her reply brought a quiver of a smile to his lips. 'Neither am I,' he added, banging on the door with his cane, and a woman wearing white scrubs appeared.

'My nurse,' he said, his lip curling at the description. 'Or what passes for a nurse these days.'

'What can I say? There were no oil lamps left,' she said, casting a professional eye over her patient and detecting the signs of strain in his face.

'Have you thought of using a wheelchair?'

Two pairs of eyes swivelled Lizzie's way.

Ah, well, she thought philosophically, she had to say the wrong thing at some point.

'The last person who said that got this cane thrown at them.'

'Wow, I can see where your grandson got his tolerant disposition from.'

The old man fought off a smile. 'At least you have good child-bearing hips!'

It was so outrageous that Lizzie laughed, and before she could denounce this sexist comment he vanished through the doors, leaving the nurse to throw an apologetic look over her shoulder.

Did that go well?

Lizzie wouldn't go that far, but it hadn't gone badly as such, she decided as she began to retrace her steps. She passed musicians carrying their instruments on the way and by the time she reached the dining room it had emptied.

The only person there was Adonis, who was seated at the piano that lived there, his fingers moving quite professionally across the keys. The moment he saw her, his fingers came crashing down on the keys with a discordant clatter.

He rose and walked quickly across to her.

'The party broke up early?'

'It did.'

'Can't say I'm not relieved.'

'So how did it go?'

'You mean did I say the wrong thing?'

'No, I mean how did it go?' He could hardly blame her for doubting his concern was genuine. It came as a shock to him as well.

'It was OK, I think, right up to the moment I suggested a wheelchair.'

Amusement sparked in his dark eyes. 'Did he throw anything at you?'

'No, he just told me I had good child-bearing hips.'

The comment drew his eyes straight to the area in question, where her tight bottom was lovingly outlined beneath the heavy smooth fabric that he had noticed flowed in an arousing way when she moved. Who was he kidding? There didn't need to be flowing involved. She just aroused him, full stop. Maybe it was the fact she made no attempt to seduce that made her inherent sexiness all the more powerful?

He had to admit that powerful barely covered the hunger she had awoken in him. He felt he was hovering on the edge of a loss of self-control continually.

The knowledge she was a virgin should have simply drawn a very clear line in the sand. Instead it was a very faint line that he kept making rational excuses to step over. Without the disturbing, yet also, he had to admit, arousing virgin tag hanging over her he would have skipped tonight altogether and they would have spent it in bed.

'I think that was meant as a compliment.'

'I didn't take it that way.' Despite her claim, she gave a tolerant smile. 'And anyway, it's probably true.' She sighed as her eyes flickered to the piano. 'You play well.'

'No, I play adequately,' he said, a half-smile tugging at his lips. He retrieved the jacket he had slung across the back of a chair and shrugged it on.

'How very self-deprecating of you.' She stopped, shock flickering into her eyes. She was teasing Adonis Aetos. It was strange, she reflected, how quickly their relationship had developed.

'You made an impression tonight.'

'Good, bad, indifferent?'

'The consensus appears to be that I am a lucky man.'

She felt the heat climb to her cheeks.

He studied her face. 'Why do compliments make you so uneasy.'

'They saw the clothes, not me.'

'They saw you, in these clothes, which is quite different,' he retorted, standing aside to let her walk through the door before him. 'Lizzie, I think it's time you let that miserable little girl who was teased by stupid boys and jealous girls go.'

She stared at this cool analysis of her teenage years, opening her mouth and then closing it again.

'Does the therapy come with the rings? Or do I pay extra? I didn't mean in bed or anything,' she said, digging herself deeper into a mire of confusion. 'Obviously not. I wasn't suggesting—'

He looked at her, and the hard expressionless stare sent her stomach into free fall. 'I know you weren't.' If he hadn't known about her inexperience, he would be wondering about it now. 'It's free, no strings.'

She brought her lashes down in a concealing fringe as she fell into step beside him.

'I'd never find my way back on my own.'

'I'll give you the guided tour tomorrow. You'll soon find your way around.'

He turned on a lamp and the room was immediately flooded with soft golden light. Lizzie stood there, nerves jangling. 'Where is that cat?'

'Do you want a drink?'

She shook her head. 'Best not.'

He nodded and moved away, she was not sure where to, but the tension went with him. When he came back a few minutes later, she was standing where he had left her, statue still.

'If you are still looking for the cat, she is asleep on my cashmere sweater.'

'Oh, no!' She gasped with a horror way out of proportion to the situation. 'I will go and get her—'

He caught her arm as she rushed past him, spinning her around to face him.

'Leave it, she's fine where she is.'

For a long moment, neither moved. Tension zigzagged in the air between them.

Her eyes were drawn to the contracting ripple of muscle in his brown throat before he released her arm.

She didn't step away.

She didn't breathe.

'Will you stop looking at me like that?' he ground out.

'Like what?' Her throat felt achy. She could only whisper.

'Like you're seeing us naked in bed.'

'I wasn't, but I am now.' Her own boldness shocked her.

His eyes darkened. Her honesty was a massive aphrodisiac. 'And how does that make you feel?' he asked, his voice low and sinfully seductive as he bent in close enough for her to feel the warmth of his breath on her cheek, close enough to make her head spin.

Could a person forget how to breathe? she wondered as she stood frozen, her heart pounding as he bent his head. There was no barrier as he slid his tongue between her lips before plunging it in deep, the action drawing a keening sound from her throat.

The heat between them was instantaneous.

Lizzie rose on her tiptoes, her hands sliding up his back, feeling ridges of muscle before she raised her arms to link her fingers behind his neck. As she kissed him back, pressing in closer, a wild, inarticulate need pulsed through her body.

As the kiss grew frantic there was nothing in her head but burning need, nothing but his muscles and hot hard body, the male scent of him, the heat of him.

Breathing hard, Adonis broke the kiss and, looking into her glazed blue eyes, placed his hands on her narrow waist. Her half-closed eyes flickered wide when he lifted her off the ground as though she weighed nothing.

Reacting on instincts she hadn't known she possessed, Lizzie automatically wound her legs tight around his waist, the action dragging words of approval from his lips.

They made a staggering progress backwards through the open door, mouths still sealed as they kissed frantically.

Lizzie was shocked by the primal ferocity of the need that coursed through her, shocked and excited as her heart thudded like a hammer against her breastbone as he laid her down on the bed.

Panting, she stared up at him, the raw power he exuded overwhelming.

'You sure about this?'

She nodded, not trusting her voice.

He knelt beside her and brushed the hair from her face, the tenderness contrasting with the fierce glow in his deep-set eyes. Somehow the fact his hand was shaking made her feel safer, the knowledge that this wasn't just happening to her.

She turned her head and pressed an open-mouthed kiss into his palm.

'I need to hear you say it.'

She reached up and framed his face with her small hands. 'I want this. I want you.'

He lowered his head again, and this time she met the thrust of his tongue.

His chest heaving, he pulled back. 'One taste of you would never be enough.'

Emotion lodged in her throat, and she pushed her reply past the aching occlusion. 'You can have as much of me as you want.'

With a growl he covered her beautiful, sensuous mouth, feeding the flames with every stroke and thrust of his tongue, every greedy nip and clash of teeth.

She gasped and twisted as his hands slid under her dress, along the soft smooth skin of her thighs. His hands felt cool on her overheated skin.

He suddenly pulled her into a sitting position, one hand on the small of her back.

'You look beautiful in this dress, but I really want to see you without it.'

The idea of being naked in front of the most beautiful man on the planet ought to have set off warning bells in her head, but it didn't.

Dry-throated with anticipation, she lifted her bottom as, holding her eyes, he tugged at the fabric until it bunched around her thighs, then pulled it off in one swipe over her head and, not taking his eyes off her for a second, threw it over his shoulder.

The way he stared at her, the searing heat, made her feel as though he were staring right into the heart of who she was. When he pressed a hand to her chest she fell back bonelessly, her heart thudding as she waited for him.

'You're beautiful,' he rasped, feasting his eyes on the soft pale curves of her body, the full breasts inside the lace covering, the flare of her hips and the lovely line of her slim, shapely legs. Thinking about them wrapped around him while he was inside her raised his internal temperature a few more painful degrees.

Adonis was a man who prided himself on being in control of every aspect of his life, but as he stared down at her so hard his vision blurred he didn't even try to pretend he was in control.

He'd thought he knew sex, loved the uncomplicated simplicity of it, but this was not the sort of sex he was used to.

It was raw. His feelings were raw. It was different and not just because he was her first—the difference was in him. It was as if her vulnerability connected with something in him that he hadn't known was there. This level of intimacy was beyond anything he knew.

The knowledge made him hesitate but only for a second. The need in him was too strong. His breath escaped in a deep shuddering sigh that lifted his chest and made the sinews in his neck stand out.

She watched as he stood up, pulling at his own clothing, weak with lust as he stripped until he stood there wearing just a pair of boxers.

There was not an ounce of surplus anything. He was all hard, sculpted muscle, lean sinew and strength, the essence of masculinity. Golden and utterly, absolutely perfect. Looking at him made the muscles in her pelvis tighten and her nipples tighten and peak.

She reached up as he came to kneel on the bed beside her, her palms flat on his damp skin, loving the firm texture and fascinated by the iron hardness. Reacting to a primal need, she pulled herself up to taste the salt on his chest, sliding her arms around his back to support herself as she licked lower and felt dizzy with power as a groan was ripped from some place deep in the barrel of his chest.

She was barely aware of him unclipping her bra, not until he began to peel it from her shoulders and her full breasts spilled free. She gave a voluptuous little shudder as he stared, rapt, at the quivering globes of flesh.

'Theos...' he groaned, bending his head to take one pink pouting nipple into his mouth.

The scalding pleasure made her back arch. Her fingers sank into his hair, then he pushed her back onto the tumbled bedclothes, the first skin-to-skin contact as his chest crushed her sensitised breast, his hair-roughened legs pushing into her thighs, was beyond anything she had imagined.

She pushed against him to increase the friction as they kissed, triggering a frantic, feverish battle of clashing tongue and teeth.

As he lifted slightly off her, her protest turned to a low keening cry as he began to slide down her body, leaving an erotic trail of open-mouthed kisses, of clever caresses, until it felt as though every nerve ending in her body were screaming.

When he reached the apex of her legs, the soft curls there, she realised that she was wrong—there were more nerve endings, more of everything.

'You're so hot and ready for me,' he whispered into her ear as he slid a finger deeper into her while continuing to rub the sensitised throbbing nub with his thumb.

Her hand slid down his belly. His skin was damp with sweat. 'I want…' she husked.

'You will, you will. I'll show you everything I like, but now I can't take any more of this,' he rasped, shaking with need. He had never wanted a woman this much in his life before.

As he slid a knee between her legs she opened up for him, tensing slightly as the silky hard tip of his erection nudged her hot, sensitive flesh. But as he whispered things she had never imagined any man saying to her she relaxed, and when he entered her slowly it was a relief and then so much more.

As his big hands cupped her bottom, exerting fierce control, each stroke sent her deeper into herself, the pleasure like a drug as, snug inside her, he continued to move.

He held on until he felt the first contraction of her body around him and then let go.

He watched her face as her body slowly relaxed, her eyelashes fluttering like butterfly wings against her flushed cheeks. She opened her glowing eyes and looked at him, gave a smile, and he felt himself captured totally by some emotion he had never experienced before.

She lay there panting while he removed the condom she hadn't even been aware of him putting on. When he rolled back to her she snuggled into him, laying her head on his chest.

She felt him stiffen but only for a moment. His arms came around her and she sighed out her pleasure.

'Who needs love,' she said happily, 'when you have sex?'

She had verbalised pretty much his philosophy on life but for some reason he felt a chink of dissatisfaction slide into his afterglow.

CHAPTER NINE

LIZZIE SURFACED FROM a deep sleep and stretched, cat-like, relaxed until the events of the night filtered into her sleep-soaked head. She tensed and slowly opened her eyes, lighting on an empty pillow beside her on the bed.

An overwhelming sense of loneliness swamped her, which was crazy. She'd been waking up alone all her life. Last night had been incredible but she had to keep it in proportion. She couldn't act like a teenager who had discovered sex and felt as though she was brilliant at it.

Which she was.

Reviewing last night, beyond the pleasure and his utter gorgeousness was the total lack of inhibition she had felt. After a lifetime of hating her body she had actually discovered it was possible to like it, love it even, because Adonis gave every indication that he did.

Whatever happened in the future she would

always be grateful to Adonis for breaking her free of her self-imposed prison. She pushed the thought away, not keen on thinking too far ahead, determined to enjoy the moment. It would be a much nicer moment if Adonis were here.

As she felt the cold bed beside her, she remembered him saying at some point during the long night that he had arranged to speak to his grandfather's doctor this morning.

She prised herself from the warmth of the bed and walked through to the bathroom where Mouse was lying full-stretch on the heated marble floor, purring.

She smiled. Inside, she was purring too.

She stepped into the shower and stood there for a long while letting the jets of water ease the tightness in muscles that were complaining, muscles she hadn't known she possessed until last night.

She brushed out her wet hair but couldn't work up the enthusiasm to do anything to it, and, after applying some suncream, she glossed her lips and left it at that. Even barefaced, her dark brows framed her face, and the natural dark of her lashes intensified the colour of her eyes.

For the first time in her life she looked in the mirror and felt lucky. Humming softly to herself, she dressed quickly, selecting a pair of linen wide-legged trousers from her new wardrobe and topping them with a square-necked white tee shirt. She shoved her feet into a pair of leather sliders and, calling the cat, walked into the sitting room.

The first thing she noted after she opened door to a generous enclosed green space, where stone benches were set around what appeared to be a herb garden, was a note propped on the table. She bent down to pick it up while the cat wound his way around her legs.

Sorry I had to leave. I fed the cat. See you for breakfast.

There were no kisses attached to the note, just his name written in a bold flourish. The idea of him feeding her cat made her smile. If miracles carried on happening with this sort of regularity, where would they be in a week?

She hoped in bed. She had a lot of years of abstinence to make up for.

'So come on, Mouse, let's go for a walk, sweetheart. See if there are any local felines you need to show who's boss.'

As if she understood every word, the cat fell in by her side, tail high as they walked down the corridor. She found the dining room from the previous night and gave a self-satisfied smile, hoping, as she pushed open the door, this was where she was meant to be.

It was. Several family members from the previous evening were already there.

'*Yassas,*' she said. It had seemed only polite to learn a couple of Greek words, but she had almost exhausted her vocabulary.

'*Yassas,*' came the group reply, which seemed a positive response to her effort.

'Coffee is there.' One of the older twin girls pointed to the long low serving table down one wall. There were jugs of juices, platters of breads, bowls piled high with fruit, thick, creamy Greek yogurt and pots of honey, and that was before she had looked under the domed lids of the multitude of serving dishes.

'I can call for fresh tea,' her twin added. 'If you want some and if you need anything fresh cooking, just say.'

'We do self-service on the holidays,' Lydia explained, sounding apologetic. 'Did you sleep well?' she asked as Lizzie picked the lid off a bowl of creamy-looking scrambled egg.

'Mum, of course she didn't sleep.' The teenagers giggled, rolling their eyes at their mother.

To Lizzie's relief, Mouse provided a distraction just by being herself.

'Get down, Mouse,' Lizzie said, pushing the marauding feline off the serving table.

'She has a cat!' exclaimed one of the diminutive twins excitedly. 'Cora, look—a cat!'

'Can we stroke him?'

'Her,' Lizzie said, smiling to see Mouse lapping up the attention plus any stray crumbs that landed on the floor.

'It might not like it, girls,' their mother warned.

'Oh, she'll love it,' Lizzie promised. 'But don't let her persuade you to feed her. She is very greedy.'

'Mouse?' said one of the older twins. 'Like the books?'

'That's cool,' added her twin.

'Did you name her after the real Mouse, the cat in the books?'

'Kind of,' Lizzie said, helping herself to some yogurt and topping it with fruit. She had it halfway to her mouth when Adonis appeared looking every kind of wonderful in faded denim shorts and a tee shirt.

'Adonis, did you know she has a cat?'

'Indeed, I did know,' he said, flashing a warm look towards Lizzie.

'She has the top of her ear missing, like the books.'

Iris and her twin exchanged looks.

'Pink nose, half an ear and the black spot on her back does look like a question mark. She is the Mouse, isn't she?'

'Which would mean,' her twin said, picking up the story, 'you would be Rose Trelawny?' She gave her head a little shake. 'Not really?'

Lizzie tried to adopt a bewildered expression but she felt the guilty heat climb to her cheeks.

'Have you two read one of Lizzie's books?'

The women in the room turned on him, eyes wide. 'You married Rose Trelawny? This is Mouse the cat?'

'Adonis, is this true?' his aunt Elena demanded.

Adonis looked bewildered. 'She isn't Rose Trelawny.'

'My middle name is Rose and Trelawny was Mum's maiden name. I told you I wrote books.'

'Oh, my God, Adonis!' said Areti. 'She is so way, way out of your league.'

'Will someone tell me what the hell is going on?'

'Rosie's adventures, are they based on real life?'

'Areti!' gasped her mother, who had read the book. Despite her outrage, she could not hide her interest in Lizzie's reply.

'I was just asking, Mum. Did you really have sex in a cupboard, Lizzie, or should we call you Rosie?'

'Lizzie.'

'Sex in a cupboard,' echoed Lydia's youthful lover, who had strolled into the room. 'Wouldn't there be a space issue?'

'Depends how flexible you are...' his lover pointed out.

'Mum, ugh!'

Adonis leaned back and watched as his bride fielded questions about the heroine all present seemed to assume was her alter ego.

Lizzie had had very little contact with fans before, outside online reviews, and she had preserved her anonymity, which made it a lot easier to laugh off the more out-there questions. Being pelted up close and personal was proving difficult.

'No, he was fictional. I've never dated anyone as awful as Damien and he really wasn't that awful.'

'Are you kidding? He was a f—'

'Areti!' warned her mother.

The girl grinned.

Finally she'd had enough.

'Adonis, make it stop!'

Adonis rose to his feet. 'Right, you lot, out.

This woman has not finished a meal since she arrived and she gets very cranky when she is hungry. Also, stop feeding that cat!'

'She's hungry!' his little cousins protested.

'No, she is an opportunist. Out!'

'If you're not careful she will put you in her next book,' was Areti's parting shot.

'You were very rude, but thanks.'

'Eat,' he said, taking a seat opposite Lizzie.

'You're not eating.'

'I already have.'

'You had your meeting with the doctor?'

He set his elbows on the table. 'I did.'

'Don't stare like that, it puts me off my breakfast.'

'Not noticeably,' he drawled, the laziness in his voice as he watched her scoop a spoonful of yogurt into her mouth in dramatic contrast to the dark hunger in his eyes.

'So, the doctor?'

'Later.'

She studied his face and noticed the shadow under his eyes, which added to, not detracted from his general gorgeousness. They might not be entirely due to a long athletic sleepless night. She felt a sharp stab of empathy. She had been only a child but she remembered all too well how much her dad had dreaded his meetings with the doctors.

'My mum was ill for a long time. I was young but I know my dad grew to dread the doctor's appointments.'

'It was early onset dementia?'

She nodded. 'Yes… We kind of lost her bit by bit. It was hard as a kid to understand why she did the things she did.'

'I'm sorry,' he said, something twisting hard in his chest when he thought about Lizzie, a little girl, watching her mother vanish and her father so wrapped up in his own grief that she was left to sink or swim.

'Maybe that's why you have such a vivid imagination. You escaped into a fantasy world?'

'I never thought of that, I suppose little bits of yourself do come out in your writing…' she mused. 'Once,' she began, then shook her head. 'There are lots of good memories too.'

'So, my family seem convinced that your stories are based on personal experience. A cupboard,' he said suddenly. 'Really?'

She gave a gurgling laugh and then sobered. 'Once I got locked in a cupboard, so I let my heroine have sex in a cupboard…sort of therapy. It didn't work though. I still hate enclosed spaces.'

'But not sex.'

A slow smile illuminated her face. It faded when she found herself wondering if it was just sex or sex with Adonis.

'No, not sex,' she said quietly. 'So thank you for that, Adonis.'

'No thanks are required, I promise you, *yineka mou*.'

She stared at him, a question in her big blue eyes, a question he didn't want to acknowledge even to himself.

'The famous cat is eating the smoked salmon.'

She leapt to her feet. 'Oh, no…bad girl.' She shooed the cat away from the dish, and Mouse jumped down, retreated to a corner and gave her a dirty look.

'So you are famous?'

She looked uncomfortable and arched a brow. 'I really hope not.'

'Why didn't you tell me?'

'I did,' she protested.

'The lie was in the omission. Why do you downplay your achievements?'

'I don't…' She caught his eye and dragged a hand across her brow before shaking her head, the action causing her high ponytail to flick.

'Your father must be proud of you.'

'He is.' She heard the shrill insincerity in her voice and winced.

'My dad wanted a son. Don't get me wrong, he has always loved me and been a good dad, but I gave up trying to impress him a long time ago. You pick your battles, the ones that matter, the ones you can win.'

'I've not noticed you showing much restraint when it comes to arguing with me.'

'Oh, that's because I know I can always win those arguments. Right being on my side.'

Her pert response drew a throaty laugh from him. 'Is that a fact?'

'It is.'

'So will you put me in a book as one of your long line of loser boyfriends?'

'You're not my boyfriend.' He was her husband. Even after last night that reality felt too surreal to put into words.

'No, I'm not, am I? Perhaps it could be the start of another bestselling series. The husbands my cat warned me about.'

'It is fiction, comedy… Besides, my cat approves of you, and I haven't had a long line of boyfriends, loser or otherwise. It is fiction, you know, made up,' she mocked gently.

'This bestseller list must have made you a rich woman?'

'I don't know—well, obviously I know I've made money. I told you I bought the house. I have an agent and accountant who handle that side of things. I did run the idea past them of helping dad,' she admitted. 'But they said the bulk of my investments can't be touched without six months' notice.'

If she believed them, who was he to disabuse her? If she had known the first thing about finances she might not have spent last night in his bed.

'If you want to talk about whatever it was the doctor said...'

He tipped his head and got up. 'You finished with the food?'

She nodded.

'You said you worked in a stable so presumably you ride?'

'I do.'

'Then how about a horseback tour of the island?'

A smile spread across her face. It made him think of the sun rising.

'I can only see one issue...the cat? Can you bear to be parted from her?' He arched a brow, a smile that made her heart flip hovering across his lips.

'Do not let appearances deceive you. Admittedly she is slightly overweight, but my Mouse is an alpha cat. She will want to establish her supremacy and also find the kitchen, where she will give a very good impression of a starving animal. Mouse is a survivor.'

'So are you.'

She blinked and pushed out an embarrassed, 'I'm fine.' The idea she had painted herself as some sort of victim horrified her.

'I know you are. Go get changed. We are going for a ride. I have a couple of things to sort—shall we say half an hour in the stables? I'll get Georgiou to show you the way.'

She had no idea who Georgiou was, but she nodded her agreement.

CHAPTER TEN

THE BOOTS WERE her own but she was pretty sure that the jodhpurs, which clung in all the right places, had not been there when she left for breakfast. She suspected that one of the twins might have donated them but she decided not to question the appearance in case they had belonged to another personal female guest he had brought to the island.

She didn't want to dwell on the idea, but it was too late. She had left the suite but she had to go back and change, exchanging the borrowed jodhpurs for a pair of jeans. They were less clingy in a sexy way than the discarded jodhpurs but she didn't feel queasy wearing them.

Georgiou turned out to be an enthusiastic young man who was working the holidays before he started university. He was a mine of personal information, and by the time she got to the stables—a quadrangle of purpose-built buildings housing some impressive-looking animals who watched her from their stalls— Lizzie knew all about Georgiou's ambitions in life, and the life story of his sister, who was on a dance scholarship funded by the Aetos family and, according to her fond brother, a future prima ballerina.

The boy saw Adonis a little after Lizzie had spotted the tall, elegant figure who was wearing a white open-necked shirt, his long legs encased in snug-fitting jeans and the boots polished but well-worn.

The boy waved and left as Lizzie walked towards Adonis, who was holding two horses. The taller of the two, a black Arab, was pawing the ground, the smaller, a delicate mare with a blaze, seemed much more placid.

'So you can ride? Not like donkeys-on-a-beach ride?'

'I love donkeys.'

'I thought you might,' he said, silently adding dogs with missing limbs, anything ugly, animals that were blind, and literally anything rejected by anyone else. Lizzie Rose's perception of the world was like learning another language.

It conflicted with any perception he had ever

had, and yet at the same time was oddly attractive.

'She is beautiful,' Lizzie exclaimed, softening her voice as she stroked the soft muzzle and murmured approval to the little mare with the blaze. 'Beautiful girl.'

He handed her a hard hat, which she fastened. 'Want a leg-up?'

She nodded and found herself boosted into the saddle.

Beside her she could see Adonis control his horse gently with skill. He was totally in tune with the animal, in harmony rather than control. The two moved as one, and his attitude relaxed as the high-spirited animal caracoled.

Adonis's last remaining concerns faded as he saw her in the saddle. As he looked at her he felt the neat, emotionless boundaries that had always been in place with the women in his life dissolve. His expression sobered as he recognised the danger. The last thing in the world he wanted was a relationship with no boundaries, the sort of relationship that his parents shared.

His horse broke into a canter, and behind him he was aware of Lizzie catching up with him. She flashed him a smile that didn't seem at all dangerous, a smile full of just the joy of the moment and utterly uncomplicated.

After an hour they had covered a lot of ground and a dozen terrains. She remarked on this to Adonis when they paused to stare at a particularly spectacular vista.

'Yes, the island packs a lot into a small area.'

'It's very beautiful. I can see it must have been a marvellous place for a child to grow up.'

He touched the rim of the leather herder's hat he wore, a hat that hid his eyes from her view.

'In those days, a long way away from medical assistance when you break an arm, or a leg, or have a concussion.'

'Sounds like you were reckless.'

'Grandfather's attitude was if it hurts you won't do it again and if you do you get zero sympathy.' Without a word he dismounted.

Lizzie followed suit and stood there, reins in hand.

'The doctor tells me there is a clinical trial. A new drug or combination of them.'

'A cure!' she exclaimed.

'No, not a cure, but for patients at stage four it can mean a significant extension of life.'

'Well, that's good, isn't it?'

'Apparently, the old man doesn't think so. The doctor has asked me to persuade him, but the thing is… Do I have that right? He has been through a lot of treatments and not all pleasant,' he added with a sombre laugh. 'A man should decide his own fate.'

Her heart ached for the moral dilemma that was clear on his face.

He swept the hat off his head and a lock of hair fell in his eyes. 'I shouldn't be asking you this. It's not your problem, except of course it does affect you. If my grandfather lives longer you would stay married to me for longer.'

She flinched as though he had struck her. 'When have I ever given you a reason to think I am that sort of person?'

He turned and tilted her face up to him. 'Never. I know you are not that sort of person, but I am. I am selfish and I have to own that the idea of having you in my bed for longer makes it hard for me to stay objective about this.' He unfastened her helmet and pulled it off. 'It is good, isn't it, the sex?'

She nodded, not understanding why the acknowledgement should make the emotional tears rise up in her throat. Without a word he took the reins from her hand and tethered both horses loosely on a nearby branch. Returning to her, he took her hand and led her to a spot where the moss was deep and springy.

Turning her to face him, he kissed her. She could feel him shaking with the strength of his restrained passion. Together they sank to the ground.

'You must be sore…last night…'

She shook her head and wordlessly took his hand, fitting it to her breast.

It was slow and so tender that she cried when it was over, her head against his heart, hearing the sound of the life force in him and realising she had fallen in love with a man who did great sex but not love. His heart still belonged to Deb. Would it always?

'What's wrong?' he asked, levering himself into a sitting position as she paused in the act of gathering her clothes.

Lizzie froze and turned her head towards him.

When you make love to me…you don't kind of close your eyes and think of Deb, do you?

For one horrific split second she thought she had said the words out loud.

'What's wrong?' he repeated, his frown deepening.

Lizzie shook her head.

'Nothing… I think something stung me,' she prevaricated.

'I didn't hurt you.'

She paused in the act of fastening her bra. 'No, of course not.'

His frown smoothed, relief sliding through him, though he searched her face, horrified at an almost visceral level at the idea of hurting her.

Lizzie was fully dressed by the time Adonis had retrieved his shirt. He continued to watch her as he fastened it.

'You sure you are all right?'

She nodded as she clambered over a large rocky outcrop.

'Be careful,' he called out sharply. 'There's a drop.'

Lizzie had already taken several steps back. 'So I see,' she said as he joined her, his shirt still hanging loose.

'It's beautiful!' she said, staring from a safer distance at the ocean stretched below, blue hitting the blue of the horizon.

The light touch on her shoulder broke her free of her transfixed contemplation of the dazzling seascape.

They retraced their steps and Adonis bent low to sweep up his discarded hat.

'I love horses,' she said, leaning low over her mount's mane to pat her shoulder when they were both back in the saddle. 'Honestly, if you had ever seen how much confidence it can give a kid who feels like an outsider.'

'You?'

'Gosh, no,' she disclaimed immediately. 'The stables I help out at work with children with disabilities. In a wheelchair people look down at them, in the saddle they are equal.'

'You understand people who feel like outsiders?'

She flicked him a look from under her lashes, not liking his perception. 'Should we be getting back?'

'Are you going to tell me what's wrong?' he asked, looking down into her face. 'You were going to say something back there.'

'You never talk about Deb, and I understand it must be hard, but I just wanted to say,' she continued with a small, understanding smile of encouragement, 'that I can listen. I mean, if you wanted to, talking helps sometimes, remembering the good bits.'

He stared down at her, his expression inscrutable. 'I don't want to talk about Deb.'

She immediately felt embarrassed. The sex was so intense it had created an illusion that they were much closer than they were. His closed-off expression was ample proof they were not.

'No, of course not. I'm… Well, I'm here. Thanks.'

CHAPTER ELEVEN

THE TWO TEENAGERS hugged their grandfather before they ran around the table to where Lizzie sat nibbling at a piece of toast. She got to her feet and was swallowed up in a hug.

'I can't believe the summer is over!' Areti, her skin tanned to a deep gold, cried as she pulled Lizzie in for another hug. 'God, school next week!' she moaned. 'I can't bear it.'

Her twin rolled her eyes and took her turn hugging Lizzie. 'Listen to her. She loves it, captain of everything going, whereas I—'

'Are a swotty nerd.'

'Granted,' her twin acknowledged with a grin. 'Our last year. Next year we will be free spirits or more likely terrified of starting uni.'

Lizzie remembered her last term at school. The sixth year had been less traumatic than her early years and by then her main tormentor, Deb, had left. The invitation to a holiday with the cool girls had made her feel her life had changed. Then her bikini top had pinged off. She should have laughed it off, she could see that now. But she hadn't had the twins' confidence so instead she had layered up and never really stopped layering until she had seen herself through Adonis's eyes.

She wanted to say 'don't wish your life away' to the twins, which made her feel very old, but she restrained herself.

'You'll come and wave us off?'

'Of course,' Lizzie promised, retaking her seat.

The room seemed still after the girls' exit. The place was going to seem empty after the summer bustle of activity. Elena had taken Cora and Chloe back at the beginning of the week and all the men had gone back last week.

It was hard to believe that she had been here seven weeks.

Though Adonis had made several trips back to London and to Athens he had spent every night, or what was left of it, in her bed.

He was working from here, establishing his work base in an office away from his private suite.

'Less distractions,' he had said.

They spent a lot of time together swimming and riding, making love. They were idyllic moments she would always treasure. Thinking of them ending was the only cloud on her horizon.

'Are you going to eat that?'

Lizzie, shocked out of her dreamy contemplation of the plate she had piled with scrambled egg, looked up and found Spyros staring at her from his place at the head of the table.

Everyone had been delighted when, without any prompting, he had decided to take part in the treatment trial, which he appeared to be, as the doctor had phrased it, 'tolerating well'. That, along with his new pain regime, had put him in a much more mellow frame of mind—mellow for him anyway—and the fact he had agreed to use a motorised wheelchair meant he was much more mobile.

'I've had enough,' she said lightly, aware that the shrewd eyes fixed on her missed very little.

'You haven't had any.'

She waved her piece of toast and smiled. 'Filled up on toast.'

Spyros grunted. Since he had discovered that Lizzie was, as he put it, an adequate chess player, she saw him most days outside the noisy communal mealtimes and she'd grown very fond of him.

'You want to continue our game later?'

She gave an apologetic smile. 'Maybe not

today. I'm feeling slightly off colour,' she admitted, not quite meeting his beady eyes. 'I'll just go and see them off.'

'You do that.'

'Adonis is sorry he couldn't see you off,' Lizzie said, embracing Lydia as the remainder of their luggage was stowed on the jet.

'Don't worry, he said goodbye this morning.' She took Lizzie by the arms. 'We are all so happy he has you. You do know that?'

Lizzie didn't say anything. What could she say that wasn't a lie or, even worse, the truth?

With a sigh she gave a last wave to the faces in the window of the plane and got into the waiting car.

She didn't go up to the house, instead she went to the beach. Over the weeks they had fallen into a daily pattern. Adonis tried to make himself free around this time and they swam in the warm blue water or sometimes just walked and talked.

It would have been easy for anyone watching to think they were a happily married couple for real.

She stripped off her blue cambric sundress, underneath which she wore a blue bikini.

She wandered down to the water's edge, not

wading in, just allowing the waves to gently break over her feet. She closed her eyes, allowing the image of Adonis, bare-chested in a pair of cut-off denims, to form in her head.

It was so vivid that when she opened them she was shocked he wasn't standing there.

Enough of this, she decided, her chin lifting as her expression became resolute. She couldn't keep delaying. She had to know.

Half an hour later she was standing staring at her own pale face in the mirror, the third test strip in her hand. It wasn't really a shock, she'd suspected it for a full week—longer, even. All the signs had been there.

The irony was she had what Deb had wanted: Adonis's wedding ring on her finger and now his baby.

Except she didn't have his heart. That still belonged to Deb. Her face crumpled as a sob gathered in her tight chest. She pressed a hand to her flat belly, realising after weeks of denial that that was what she wanted: his heart.

She loved her husband.

The harsh hybrid sound that emerged from her pale lips was part sob, part laugh.

She loved her husband, and she wanted her mum, but she couldn't have either. She sniffed and pulled her shoulders back. This was her problem and she had to deal with it.

How would Adonis react?

She pushed away the question. She couldn't deal with that now. This was happening to her. She had to sort out her own thoughts before she faced him. She would tell him, obviously, but… but…he'd stay with her because of the baby, she was sure of it, and that wasn't enough.

She pressed a hand to her head, which felt as though it were going to explode. She needed space.

The thought had barely formed when her phone pinged. She saw the name and shook her head, then, her expression thoughtful, she picked it up and read the text.

It was pretty much a repeat of the previous half-dozen she had received from her publisher, detailing the PR tour for her latest book they were trying to sell her on.

'Why are you sitting in the dark?'

Lizzie blinked when one of the bedside lights was switched on.

'What's happened? What's wrong?' His concern growing, Adonis's glance moved from Lizzie's pale face to her clothes. She was fully dressed. 'It's half one. I thought you'd be in bed.'

'Sorry, I lost track of time. I've only just finished packing,' she said brightly.

'Packing?' The dark hooded glance shifted to the bags lying on the floor and the cat sitting in its basket.

She nodded. 'Yes, it's so exciting. They want me to do a PR tour for the new book and I thought, well, I've been here a lot longer than either of us anticipated, which is great, but Spyros is on the new course of treatment and I'll be back before you know it.'

'You'll be back?' he said in a voice wiped clean of any emotion, and then, in a voice that was no longer empty, instead filled with fury, he continued, 'So how long have you been planning this?'

'Not planning. It just kind of happened.'

'We had a deal.'

'I know,' she said miserably. 'But things have changed.'

'I haven't changed.'

'I know.'

That was the problem: he hadn't changed. He still loved Deb, and Lizzie would always be second best. She really didn't want her baby to have a second-best mum.

'I thought you were happy.'

She said nothing. How could she be happy when she loved a man who didn't love her back?

Her silence fed the outrage, the sense of betrayal building inside him. He had trusted her and she had thrown that trust back in his face.

'Fine! Go. I'll get the jet fuelled up. It is at your disposal. I'll get a driver to take you to the—'

'Everyone is asleep, Adonis.'

'Then they can wake up!'

'I want to say goodbye to your grandfather.'

After a moment of nostril-quivering, jaw-clenching staring he gave a curt nod. 'As you wish.' And he was gone, leaving Lizzie to cry with no one but Mouse to hear her muffled sobs.

Lizzie snatched a few hours of uneasy sleep and woke early to throw up. So far pregnancy did not have a lot to recommend it, she decided as she examined the dark panda shadows circling her puffy eyes.

Had Adonis, true to his word, organised the jet?

She didn't have a clue. She just knew that she really couldn't face him again right now.

She knew if she had told him he'd stay married for the sake of the baby, but she didn't want that. She was not about to settle. She'd had enough of pretending.

'He doesn't love me, Mouse,' she said as she shoved the indignant cat into the travel basket and got a scratch for her troubles. 'Nobody loves me.'

Dashing the self-pitying tears from her face, she gave a loud sniff and went to the only person other than Adonis she knew could get her off the island.

She wasn't very coherent, but Spyros seemed to get the main point, which was she wanted off the island.

'The PR tour is a marvellous opportunity,' she explained brightly, hoping the concealer around her eyes was hiding the worst of the damage caused by her tears.

'Couldn't Adonis organise that for you? Didn't he get back last night?'

'He said he would, he might have, but he might have forgotten, and I don't like to disturb him. He's very busy this morning, what with everything…' she said, her voice starting bright before it trailed away into a whisper.

'The jet will need refuelling.'

'Oh, will that take long?'

'It's a big plane.'

She nodded. 'But when it is ready?'

'It is at your disposal.'

'Fine and I'm sorry that…' Shaking her head, she hugged the old man before she picked up the cat basket and her rucksack.

When she had gone, Spyros pressed a buzzer that brought assistance running.

'No, I'm not dead,' he snapped. 'Get me my grandson. Tell him I'm dying if you like. I need him here now.'

Five minutes later the door was flung open and a white-faced Adonis rushed in. His eyes widened when he saw his grandfather standing there. 'I was told you were dying.'

'*Theos!*' Spyros bemoaned. 'These people take everything so literally. Well, we are all dying, some of us sooner than others, but not today.'

'What is wrong?'

'You, if you let that woman run away.'

Adonis's expression froze. 'She has work commitments.'

'You are an idiot, you know that? You can't see what is right under your nose, what everyone else in the house can see.'

'And what is that?'

'The woman is in love with you. If you don't love her back, let her go. She deserves more.'

'Our marriage, as I am sure you have worked out, is an arrangement. Love is not part of the deal.'

The old man folded his arms across his chest and raised a bushy brow. 'If you say so.'

'I do say so,' Adonis shot back, clinging to his restraint in the face of his grandfather's interference.

'Ah, well, you know best,' he said in a tone that implied the exact opposite. 'You told her about Deb dying with her lover, did you?'

'That was not relevant.'

'I can see why you feel a bit of a fool.'

Adonis clamped his jaw.

'She thinks you still love the other one, and, the way I see it, that suits you. It means you don't have to admit to your own feelings because, well, basically, you are—and I hate to say this about my own grandson—a coward.'

His face reflecting the tangled mess of emotions in his head, Adonis sank into a chair. 'She has deserted me.'

The old man smiled. He could hear the lack of conviction in his grandson's voice.

'I'm worried about her flying. She's not been looking too good most mornings for the past couple of weeks.'

Adonis's questioning gaze flew to his grandfather's face.

'Are you saying…?'

'I'm not saying anything. It's not my place.'

Adonis shot to his feet and nodded. 'It's mine, and you are a manipulative old bastard,' he observed, slanting a half-smile at his grandparent.

'Good to know I've still got it. Nurse!' he bellowed. 'I need my meds.'

'You've already had your medication.'

'This boy is upsetting me,' he said, missing plaintive by a country mile as he added, 'Your mess, you fix it, own it, or you are not the man I thought you were. Oh, and the plane will take a long time to refuel today.'

'Excuse me, but I really think your grandfather needs his rest.'

Adonis ignored the woman, tipped his head in respect towards his grandfather, and hit the ground running.

Own it. The words went around in his head on a loop as Adonis made his way to his car.

He had spent the night telling himself that when she was gone he was free and good riddance.

His satisfaction was marred by the mocking

voice in his head that said, *Free or maybe just scared*. And that voice was the truth. He could see he was a man who had been too chicken scared to invest in a relationship in his life.

Would she be there when he arrived or would he be too late? The question tormented him as he floored the accelerator.

Lizzie sat with Mouse plaintively meowing as she waited in the warm morning sun beside the runway.

With a hissing sound of exasperation, she pulled off her sun hat and put it on top of the cat carrier. 'All right. I'd ask someone if I could but there isn't anyone here!'

There was.

She hated that her heart swelled at the sight of him.

'What are you doing sitting in thirty-five-degree midday sun? You want to get heatstroke?'

'I'm leaving.'

'How? Sprout wings and fly?'

'The jet is refuelling. Your grandfather said…'

The anger and doubts suddenly fell away as he looked into her eyes, red-rimmed and blood-shot from crying. He wanted to wrap her up and keep her safe. 'My grandfather says whatever suits him but he isn't important right now. I'm an idiot,' he said.

'Yes,' she agreed.

'And I love you. I think I've loved you from the first moment I saw you.' She stared at him, wanting to hear him say it again, not letting herself believe that this was real... She had been in the sun a long time.

'You love Deb. I understand.'

He gave a hard laugh. 'I don't love Deb. I never loved Deb. I was marrying her because I didn't love her and she didn't love me, less a marriage and more a spreadsheet,' he mused, mocking himself. 'But it turned out she wasn't as clinical as it seemed. When the helicopter went down there were not two fatalities, there was a third, her long-term lover, a married man. Spyros buried the story, God knows how.'

'Is that true? Oh, God, why didn't you tell me? Why did you let me feel like second best?' she wailed.

'It was a pride thing. Deb had taken me for a fool, which I have been,' he admitted readily. 'I have never ever been in love with your cousin and you could never be second best to anyone or anything. I knew that, I think I always did, but I've spent my life staying in control. I know now that what I feel for you bears no resemblance to my parents' toxic love. You have no idea how liberating it is to know that I am nothing like them. We are nothing like them!'

'Of course we aren't.'

'Lizzie, I'm trying to tell you I love you and I want to stay married because my life without you in it looks like one dark empty road, smooth, no bumps or twists or turns. Boring. I know I've been an idiot and I hope you can forgive me... And if this PR thing is important to you, your career matters. You should do it.'

'You'd be OK with me being away for six weeks?'

'I will come with you.'

His response made her laugh. 'I forgive you, Adonis, and it's lucky you love me because you're going to be a father.' Holding her breath, she watched the emotions move across his face before settling into an expression that banished any lingering doubts about his reaction. 'Also your feelings are totally reciprocated.'

'You love me?'

'I do.'

He exhaled deeply, his eyes sliding to her flat middle, before repeating, 'You love me?'

She nodded. 'And, yes, I really am pregnant this time,' she teased as she fell into his open arms and felt them close around her.

When the long, deep, draining kiss ended he rested his forehead against hers. 'The old man was right.'

'Spyros?' She gasped, drawing away a little to angle an astonished look up into his face.

Adonis nodded, smoothing his hand around her face and gazing lovingly into her eyes. 'He implied you were pregnant. The old reprobate doesn't miss a thing.'

'I would have told you about the baby. I just needed some space to sort it in my own head first. I would never have kept the baby from you, but I didn't want to stay with you because of the baby.'

'I know that, and I know we will not be like my parents. We will always be there for him or her.'

'It's a deal.'

It seemed appropriate to seal the deal with a kiss, which was interrupted by loud cat cries.

They broke apart, Lizzie laughing at his expression. 'Just accept it. Mouse always has the last word.'

'I know my place in the scheme of things. Perhaps you can train her to carry your ring when we renew our vows here.'

'I think that might be beyond… Renew our vows? Are we going to do that?'

'I think our family deserves to have the wedding we cheated them out of, don't you, *yineka mou*? Besides, I want to show the world how beautiful my bride is.'

She sighed. She felt beautiful. 'I'm so happy I could explode.'

'Kiss me instead.'

'I can work with that!'

EPILOGUE

'HERE, YOU HOLD ATTICUS,' she said, passing the swaddled infant with the mop of dark hair to his father. The baby looked at his father with big, interested eyes. 'I just need to, yep, done,' she said as she wiped around Lucas's mouth. He didn't open his eyes.

They were very different, in personality at least. Atticus was louder, demanding attention. Lucas, five minutes older, was more placid, but when he did lose his temper he really did lose it!

Most people could still not tell them apart. Lizzie had always been able to see the subtle little differences, the angle of Lucas's eyes and the deeper dimple in Atticus's right cheek. At six months, they were even more obvious than they had been at birth.

'Have we got time to…?'

'Plenty,' her handsome husband assured her calmly. 'It's not like they can start the christening without us, or the boys at least.' His glance slid down to her shoes, lingering a little on the way on her stupendously excellent legs. 'You going to be OK in those shoes?'

'Fine,' she promised him patiently. She had grown accustomed to his overdeveloped protective instincts during the pregnancy. He was better since the birth but still inclined to see dangers that weren't there lurking around every corner.

They took their time walking up the incline to the place where Spyros had been buried the previous week.

Once he'd known the twins were on the way, he had seemed to gain a new lease of life, and the extra months the treatment had given him had meant that he had lived to see and get to know his great-grandsons.

It had been sad when he had passed away in his sleep but, as he had said when he'd got to hold the babies for the first time, it was all about continuity and, as far as he was concerned, he was holding immortality.

Lizzie handed Lucas to his father as she laid the wildflowers on the grave, which was marked with the simple cross Spyros had requested.

She straightened up and moved in close to

Adonis's side, aware of the protective warmth of his presence that made her feel shielded from any harm.

'Thank you, Spyros,' she said quietly.

In response to the unspoken question in her husband's eyes, she said, 'If he hadn't meddled and manipulated we might never have met.' The thought of that filled her with horror.

'Oh, we would have,' Adonis responded with total conviction. 'We were meant to be together. I truly believe that.' He bent his head and brushed her lips with his, then kissed both babies in his arms. 'They look like little angels, but you do realise that as soon as we walk into the church they are going to scream the place down?'

'Oh, I'd say that is a sure thing.' She laid a hand on his arm. 'You are not upset that your parents didn't turn up?'

'Not especially. Actually, not at all. I have everything I need right here.'

* * * * *